VOYEURS

Dennis James Bartel

The Gramercy Press

Voyeurs
Copyright 2018 by Dennis James Bartel

The Gramercy Press
Los Angeles, California

Grateful acknowledgement is made to the editors of the following publications in which these stories first appeared.

Aji, "On Drinking"

Northeast, "Soldiers in the Holy Land"

Pearl, "Ashram Ethics"

Pittsburgh Quarterly, "Be It Resolved"

Windsor Review, "Our Mistake"

"Soldiers in the Holy Land" was first published in a different form in the University of Virginia anthology *Vietnam Generation.*

*For Helen who gave me life,
and for Erin who gave me new
life, with love.*

VOYEURS

CONTENTS

Also by Dennis James Bartel

High'd Up (novel), 2015

The Whores of S. Hanover Street (chapbook), 2018

BE IT RESOLVED

Essel Black sat at the open window, his concession to Rachel who found his cigar smoke an insult. The cherry tip glowed in the dark. You must understand this was 1971. You must understand this was a tract of one-story stuccos staggered along a harshly-lit suburban street in the bedroom sprawl of Southern California, each house to its own fifty-by-hundred feet. Some were submerged in the deep night shade of eucalyptus trees. Others, like the Black home, presented a flat green carpet of lawn to the world. Up and down the block, television sounds could be heard: shouts, sirens, blasts of music, mechanical laughter that sounded like waves on a beach. The ice cream truck made its faint appearance in the distance, then approached slowly with its moronic chime. Essel had noted that the truck arrived on schedule every night at eight, timed to catch the neighborhood kids outside after supper. He considered this a crass manipulation.

He remembered that growing up in old Baltimore he and his friends always half-listened for the sound of the ice cream wagon, not a truck at all. (Odd how he could remember it with greater acuity now than back when it hadn't been such a long time ago.) They'd be out on a stoop or in someone's backyard, and one of them would catch the sound of hoofbeats and pull up short to listen. Sometimes it was Mr. Ice Cream Man, sometimes not. You knew for sure when you heard his tinny bell. But you never knew when. He came at all hours. You had to be quick. He wouldn't wait.

Essel blew smoke out the window. He *did* like his cigars. He liked satisfying the occasional buried urge he felt for them. This was one of his No.2 Montecristos which he kept in an ash humidor on a top bookshelf here in the study. He preferred to smoke a cigar when there were school matters to mull over. In the time it took to smoke three-quarters of a torpedo he could adequately mull over anything, and still have a quarter left to savor, provided his prostate didn't force him to abandon the tapered butt on the windowsill. Rachel forbade smoking in the john.

This evening he was mulling over which, if any, teams he should take to the

District Debate Championships in San Diego. He'd been tempted by the thought of announcing to the entire squad – sixteen of them – that no one was going because no one deserved to go; if he hadn't succeeded in teaching them forensics, at least he could teach them something about what it means to fail. Instead, he'd narrowed the list to two teams. One was his first-ranked senior team, Helen and Suzanne, whom Essel knew would not have been first-ranked on any of his squads in the sixties; and the other was his only junior team, Mike and Benjamin, who, to be kind, need not be compared with teams of the past, as they were having enough trouble with the present.

As Essel saw it, Districts was a tournament strictly for the elite, and neither of these teams could stand up against that caliber of competition. At Districts they'd face the elite from the very first round: well-polished teams from Bishop Amat and Cal Poly and other schools that year in and year out served as breeding grounds for Stanford and USC, even the Ivy League. These debaters sweated confidence inside their suits. Their handcarts were stacked with boxes of 3-by-5 evidence cards.

To be sure, Essel knew what it took to stand up to such a caliber of competition. In past years his squads sometimes performed so spectacularly well that his heart raced, and his face flushed. From one tournament to the next word got around to other coaches, whether passed on with a respectful wink or through gnashed teeth: *Beware of Essel Black's kids.*

His best squad (though there had been many good ones) was probably 1968-69. Fifteen of twenty-four were seniors. Among his favorite success stories was the first-ranked debate team, comprised of Steve Bernardino, a senior whose forceful presence (forgodsakes by the end of the school day the boy's jaw sported the bluish shadow of a heavy beard) made him the undeclared captain of the squad; and Beverly Moskowitz, a junior with a fine analytical intelligence and keen debating instincts. They established the high-water mark for the history of the forensics program by advancing in the State Championships through round after round of victories, into the quarter-finals! and winning! going all the way to the semis! before finally succumbing in a close decision to the ultimate champions, events so thrilling that Essel found himself unexpectedly short of breath on occasion for several days after. Rachel hounded him into going to see Dr. Williger, who, as always, told Essel that he was far too heavy.

"Your heart has enough to do without the added burden of so much excitement," said the doctor.

Essel, slumped on the examining table in his skivvies, replied, "So what are you saying, I should stop teaching?"

"I'm saying you should lose weight."

"My heart can take it," he said, his fingers nervously working the corner of his pale moustache. Then, seeing the foolishness of his remark, he added with a sigh, "Of course, I must lose weight."

After that sensational year of Bernardino/Moskowitz the forensics program began a strange downward slide. Within two years Essel found himself watching as his squad was humiliated week after week at small tournaments with local schools. What happened? Well there were all those graduating seniors, led by Steve Bernardino, which was a lot of talent to lose all at once. But many of those seniors had been mentors to underclass debaters. You'd expect that a few, at least one team, would develop into good debaters. Some left the program for dramatics or sports, or love, and were replaced by slow students or delinquents who saw forensics as a way to duck the English requirement (and were apparently counseled as such by the imbeciles in Administration, specifically Swain, Boys Dean), while others who stayed with forensics gradually took on the deadened look of one who has lost interest in a mundane job but hasn't the will to quit.

Even the foremost among them stopped short of her potential. Beverly Moskowitz came back to school that autumn with a faint trace of self-satisfaction detectable along the long line of her narrow jaw. She lasted only a few weeks with her new debate partner, a longtime girlfriend, then over the strong objections of her coach Mr. Black she abandoned debate to concentrate entirely on her individual event, original oratory. As her coach saw it, this decision had few if any merits. For one thing, none of the younger debaters could reap the benefits of having the squad's best debater also immersed in the proposition, sorting out questions, spearheading affirmative and negative strategies. Where was Beverly when it came to debate? And while Miss Moskowitz was indeed, as could have been predicted, excelling in O.O., any forensics coach worth his salt, and most certainly Essel Black, will tell you that the heart and soul of forensics, its hard nugget of disciplined thinking, was to be found in debate. Emotive events such as original oratory relied in large measure on acting. In any event, Beverly's coach considered it a wrongheaded decision for her to leave debate. Then again, perhaps it had not mattered to which event she put her keen young intellect. A few weeks before graduating Beverly received a scholarship to UCLA, where she would study pre-law.

But return to the present matter, thought Essel. That was then, and this is now. The air felt cool on his face. Thank goodness no one had stopped that blasted ice cream truck. He hated it when it sat in the middle of the street blaring. Some nights he'd catch himself hours later humming that moronic tune beneath his breath. So, back to the business at hand, the reason for sitting down with this satisfying Montecristo. He decided that it was inevitable that Helen and Suzanne should go to Districts. Each had joined the program in her freshman year (Helen one semester earlier than Suzanne) and so perhaps they deserved the small honor among squad members that a trip to Districts represented. Helen, a solemn girl of self-denial, had won the squad's only trophy all year (in O.O.), and Suzanne, who was more animated than Helen, with watery blue eyes and a perpetual allergic redness around her nose, had eagerly worked hard all year to improve upon her limited talents, with measurable success. Of course, they should go to Districts, even if they wouldn't fare well. That was the easy decision. It was the questionable wisdom of taking the other team, the two junior boys, that Essel had to mull over.

Mike happened to be a favorite of Rachel's from evening practices at the Black home. He was a kinetic, volatile boy. Rachel was especially taken by Mike's oral interpretation speech, which was Atticus Finch's courtroom speech from *To Kill Mockingbird*. ("In the name of God, do your duty.") At tournaments all year, for all his shouts and fist-shaking, Mike never got very far with his Atticus Finch (one judge wrote on the ballot cruelly that he sounded more like Boo Radley), but a few times he did manage to shake some classroom rafters with righteous noise and whip up excitement in other students.

As a debater Mike was erratic (some would say stark-raving). One minute he was slumped in his chair nearly asleep, seemingly out of the debate and off in a daze; the next he was pacing before the judge, tall and lanky, tow-headed, flailing his arms in gestures of indignation. His face was hard and angular, prim around the mouth, his eyes ablaze with outrage.

For Mike, the proposition under debate made no difference. Every proposition was a personal affront. Every proposition rested on moral issues. In the autumn they debated "Be it resolved: That The United States Should Withdraw Unilaterally From South Vietnam." Mike shouted and sobbed over it. Debating affirmative he was a peacenik ready to lay his body down at Kent State. Debating negative he stood shoulder to shoulder with General Curtis LeMay, shaking his fist at his opponents. On ballots, which Essel sometimes let the boys read and sometimes did not, judges often chastised Mike for "introducing personalities into the debate." Perhaps with such a highly charged proposition as this, and such a highly-strung boy as Mike, his was only likely behavior. But in the spring Mike responded with the same delirious moral certitude to the deliberately legalistic proposition "Be it resolved: That The Environmental Protection Agency Should Be Given Regulatory Powers Over Industry." How bad did it get? One time, Mike threw a chair against a blackboard. Another, at the end of a quarter-final debate, he charged the opponents' table and in full view of five observers punched a boy in the eye. Essel was one of the observers. He noted that had they won the round (and they would have won had Mike not lost his mind) it would have represented the boys' farthest advance of the year.

Conversely, there were tournaments when Mike was too tired or too dispirited to fire his indignation, and he would stare at the floor reciting pat arguments, his voice down around his knees in an indifferent monotone, as Benjamin looked on with pained eyes. Once a judge simply drew a line through Mike's section of the ballot because he had not been able to hear any of Mike's arguments.

In two years debating together with Benjamin, Mike's antics had lost a lot of debates for them. Not that Benjamin was complaining. Benjamin must have seen that Mike had also won them a few debates, and that his, Benjamin's, careful plodding and three boxes of painstakingly typed and cross-referenced evidence cards had never won them anything. Besides, he and Mike were friends.

Every few years a boy came out for forensics who had also at one time passed through the local scout troop (533) for which Rachel was a den mother. Benjamin was one. He had not been specifically in Rachel's den, so there wasn't that intimate contact, but Rachel remembered speaking with him several times and she knew him enough to observe to her husband, "The boy was growing serious prematurely."

Perhaps, thought Essel, it was wrong to send Mike and Benjamin into the mouth of Districts. He'd seen students who were beginning to see the light in their own intellectual faculties suddenly suffer too great a humiliation at the hands of a debate team of championship caliber and turn away from forensics in revulsion. Conversely, next year Mike and Benjamin would likely inherit the standing of first-ranked senior team (however dim that prospect sounded), and to Essel's thinking a taste of the competition at this level might do the boys less harm than good.

Suddenly he sensed Rachel standing behind him. He heard her breathing, almost distinguishable as a reprimand. He turned to see her bird-slender outline, like a smudge in the dark doorway, arms folded. Forgodsakes. How long had she been there? He could barely make out her face – the downturn of her lipless mouth, the pools of disdain in her eye sockets. There was nothing to say. They drew their thoughts from the same well. He knew why she was coldly watching him, and she knew that he knew.

"I'm nearly finished," said Essel, turning away to face the street. A moment later, without looking, he knew she was gone.

A man smoking in the dark at an open window. The Montecristo was down to a plug, yet Essel had not even considered another side of the question: Should he take two senior girls and two junior boys together on an overnight trip? As far as he knew (and Rachel seemed to know this too without asking), neither Mike nor Benjamin had a girlfriend. The boys' chastity was taken for granted. But Suzanne and Helen, seniors only weeks short of graduation, that was different. Essel thought maybe he should save himself the grief.

*

You must understand Essel and Rachel moved from Baltimore to this dairyland suburb after a stillborn and four miscarriages and then it became too late. You must understand they wanted an utter change, to pull up their life by the roots. It was 1955, and this new high school out on the coast looked like an opportunity.

Once there, Essel immediately set to work carving out a niche for himself by single-handedly starting a forensics program. From the first, certain members of the Administration (i.e. Swain) resisted the program as "too high brow" for a working-class high school. Resistance was seldom overt; rather, official support was withheld at every turn (i.e. a skimpy forensics line item in the Activities budget), as was official enthusiasm (i.e. conspicuous silence on the subject of forensics at faculty meetings).

"Ultimately," Essel complained to Rachel, year after year, his thin voice rising in strained irony, "there's just one way to keep it going. Win." He pronounced the word like it were a venal sin. "It's the one thing the imbeciles understand." It was unfair to the students, of course. It was anti-educational. But in time Essel had to accept it. He was not dealing with educators here, he was dealing with imbeciles. "We're supposed to compete with the wrestling team?" he railed at his wife.

Rachel listened (or didn't listen) and always agreed completely.

Administration support notwithstanding, Essel Black built his program. Forming alliances, he struck deals with other teachers by which he would speak highly of their classes to his best and brightest, and in exchange these teachers would nudge some of their own into going out for forensics. Among the teenagers who were directing their hormonal eruptions toward bettering themselves a few could usually be coaxed into the program, wherein their coach Mr. Black would drive home for them the basics of logic and argumentation, methods of building evidence files, the use of flowsheets, how to argue from analogy and antithesis, how to exploit fallacies, etc. If they grasped the basics they were also taught some of the subtler thrust and parry techniques which often made the difference between gaining or losing the advantage. And for everyone there were simple but necessary elocution exercises (*Are you copper-bottoming them, my man? No, I'm aluminuming 'em, mum*), and vocalizing exercises such as one that Essel sensed had become something of a legend among alumni of the program: holding a lit candle close to your mouth as you let the air out of your lungs with a long "ooo." The idea was to make the flame flicker but not go out.

Over the years Essel Black made it a practice whenever anyone on the forensics squad brought home a first place to personally see to it that it was printed in the school newspaper or announced at assemblies. He insisted to Swain, to the extent that he thought Swain could be persuaded by such arguments, that forensics plaques represented the same high level of achievement as athletic trophies and should therefore be included in the lunchroom display case alongside the school's glittering and cherished stick-figure football, wrestling and rifle club trophies. As Essel Black saw it, even if he had to be a pushy old bastard, at least his squads would get the recognition they deserved.

It was with the sodden knowledge that his current squad probably *did* get all the recognition they deserved (none), that two weeks later on an early Friday morning, a full hour before the school would begin to fill with students, he waited behind his desk at the front of his classroom for his four District-bound debaters to arrive. Slanted strips of sunlight shown through the slats of the awning onto the floor. Out the doorway he could see the grass – dewy and glinting like aluminum foil.

Benjamin arrived first, without a word, nodding hello.

"Morning, Benjamin," said Mr. Black. It was always Benjamin, never Ben. Sometimes, showing a streak of high-minded self-consciousness, he refused even to respond to Ben. Mike, however, often called him Benny. He was wearing the same pale blue short-sleeve shirt and paisley tie that he wore to every tournament. He had electric razor burns on his neck. He looked alert and nervous, as if he were ready to begin the debate *this instant*.

He'll be exhausted by the time we get to San Diego, thought Essel.

The boy went immediately to the evidence boxes stacked in the corner for a final check. He took stubborn care with everything. Too much stubborn care, thought Essel. At the heart of all that fidgeting with the evidence was an insecurity that stood squarely in the way of his progress. The boy could use a spoonful of Mike's wildness. Mr. Black tossed the car keys to him and said he could go ahead and load the boxes in the station wagon.

Out front, a navy-blue Impala, ablaze in the chalky sunlight, pulled up to the curb. It was a low-rider car. Helen was in the passenger seat. Essel had no idea she ran around with that lot. He had a singular dislike of low-riders. Every morning they cruised the front of the school back and forth, back and forth, so many of them it became next to impossible to get into the parking lot. Low-riders were also, simply put, a bad element to have around the school. He'd complained more than a few times to

Swain, whose job it was to police the grounds, but in vain.

The driver was an older boy with a thick black moustache and a determined expression. Looking more closely Essel thought the boy could be as much as twenty-five, forgodsakes. Helen kissed him quickly on the mouth and got out of the car. A small black bag was slung over her shoulder. She took the long way around the moist grass. Essel listened to the clik-clok of her shoes on the cement coming up the hall.

Helen, Essel imagined, would one day be a good-looking woman. She was by no means now a pretty girl, a girl who naturally stood out among others, but a girl who could when it suited her make herself look attractive. Her big round thick glasses gave her dark eyes prominence. She had smooth, black hair in an appealing, rounded cut. But she was kept from prettiness by her unrelenting solemn manner. While Essel didn't know much about Helen's life outside school, there was one rather odd thing that he did know. In her freshman year she had made it the subject of her first (and desperately awful) O.O. speech. In the 1920s her grandfather, a U.S. Marshall in rough-and-ready Sanborn County, South Dakota, committed an exceptionally violent suicide at age sixty-two after many years of an unshakable despondency. To Essel's thinking, this ancestral vein of melancholy fed Helen's character with a thin but steady flow.

As Helen entered Mr. Black asked, "Who was that?" and nodded in the direction of the long-gone Impala. He added an impish wink, so she'd see he was just teasing. "You get a ride from your father?"

Helen said nothing. She had a self-possessed, acid smile.

Suzanne arrived a moment later wearing her long hair tucked behind her ears. Her face looked disingenuously startled, as if everything caught her off-guard. Though Mr. Black had yesterday told her No, she asked again if she could drive her own car to San Diego.

"I'll be on your tail the whole way," she pleaded. "Please, kindly Mr. Black, wise coach, dear confidante." She strode smilingly toward Helen across the room, seeking support.

"I'm not riding in that thing," said Helen. Since Christmas, when Suzanne's parents had given her a car, a Pinto, Suzanne and Helen had driven to local tournaments together. Helen was merciless about "the malodorous little heap." She said that among its many faults, safety being one of them, it was ugly, and a nothing shade of pale blue. Suzanne responded by dubbing Helen "Miss Snob."

"Young lady," Mr. Black addressed Suzanne directly, "I have already answered that question." He tried to keep a cheery tone, then he saw that Suzanne had already given up on the idea and was huddling with Helen, whispering. Those two were always whispering. It was rude.

At long last, Mike arrived, barely awake. He looked somehow different, though he was dressed in his usual helter-skelter fashion – baggy brown pants, V-neck sweater with a hole at the shoulder blade the size of a pinkie, his tie in a loosened knot, its length bulging beneath the sweater. The boy dresses like Red Skelton forgodsakes, thought Essel. Mike skidded his suitcase across the floor and collapsed theatrically in his seat, dropping his head to the desk.

"Mr. Narcoleptic," said Suzanne. She sidled up to him and tousled his hair like he was a dog. Suzanne was a big one for touching. And a big one for flirtation. "Wake up, you jerkhead," she said.

Mike lifted his head and comically knuckled the crunchies from his eyes. "That's real good, Suuu-zannne. Jerkhead."

Benjamin returned from loading the evidence boxes, jiggling the keys in his palm like dice.

"Let's go," said Mr. Black, clapping his hands briskly. "We're late already. Hup hup." As he passed Mike he clapped his hands loudly near the boy's face.

Outside in the warm sun Mr. Black told them to wait and left them standing under the awning. It irritated him that he had left the house not three-quarters of an hour ago and now already.... But he had to think of the three-hour drive. He headed for the john at the end of the building. Mike let out a mock groan, but Mr. Black turned around and stared at him with disgusted disapproval. Mike gulped his groan back down. He *does* look different, thought Essel, like people look different when their portraits are reversed in a photograph; a nearly indecipherable difference. Such an odd boy, he thought.

An overweight man nearing sixty in a dark ash suit standing impatiently at a urinal. He hated this fool dribbling. His bladder wasn't full. The pressure was all in the canal blocked by the prostate. He watched his squashed reflection in the chrome pipes atop the urinal. At least there was no pain. Last year at this time the simple act of pissing had become an ordeal. Frequency, too. One day he kept track on a 3-by-5 card in his shirt pocket and was astounded when it reached thirty. When he revealed this a few days later to Rachel she emitted a high-pitched gasp of fear only too familiar to him. She collected herself and snapped at him, "I'll call Dr. Williger *myself* if you won't!" It took three months of terazosin injections for the pain to subside to a level of manageable irritation. The frequency also dropped, though he felt too foolish to count again. These days it was just something he lived with.

Standing, waiting, he told himself not to be impatient. He allowed his mind to wander. He thought about the awful beating that Mike and Benjamin would inevitably suffer. He didn't envy them the experience. But then, he smirked, he had to admit he envied them the youthful strength of their urinary canals; their freedom to produce forceful streams of precious golden fluid, forgodsakes.

*

As soon as they on the Santa Ana Freeway, Essel rolled down his window a few inches and withdrew a cigar from inside his coat. Last thing before leaving the house, when Rachel wasn't in the room, he'd slipped three cigars into his pocket. No doubt she knew he had them, perhaps felt them through his coat as they embraced good-bye and or smelled them, yet he'd felt compelled to conceal the fact. (The half-pint of J&B in his briefcase she granted him as a vaguely romantic indulgence. The cigars were another matter.) He'd chosen two long, thin, tapered Montecristo No.2s for the drive down and back, and one fat, $2, pre-Castro La Corona Churchill, in the unlikely event that Helen and Suzanne made a respectable showing, say, advancing to the fourth round. At Districts, that would be a success worthy of celebration. He pushed in the lighter on the dash with his thumb. Benjamin, sharing the front seat, glanced uninterested at the cigar and turned his face to the window.

"Mr. Black!" Suzanne said from her place in the middle of the back seat. "I'm shocked. You're not going to smoke that are you? *In the car?*"

"Nothing shocks you girls," Mr. Black replied, glancing at Helen in the rearview mirror. She was scrunched into the near corner. "Are you shocked, Helen?"

"I *am* shocked, Mr. Black," said Helen. "Mind if I have a cigarette?"

Suddenly Mike blurted out, "There's the Matterhorn!" Off to the right, nearly hidden behind a bank of trees, was

Disneyland's Magic Kingdom, the only part visible being the mighty snow-capped Alpine peak.

Suzanne, who had requested at the outset that they have the radio on, low at least, suddenly exclaimed, "Bitchin! Stevie Winwood! I really *really* like Traffic." She jerked her head to face Helen. "This sounds like the long version." Helen shrugged.

Having tuned out the noise in the car, Essel smoked his Montecristo. He thought about how every now and then he would insist to Rachel that her repugnance toward cigars was something less than empathic and remind her that she herself had once been a pack-a-day smoker. Winston's. Essel's thoughts fled back to their courtship and the puppy years of their marriage, a time when smoking had been important to them. One of their favorite pastimes in those pastoral days was to take weekend trips to Civil War battlefields in Maryland, Pennsylvania and Virginia. The battlefield names alone stirred his heart: Manassas, Antietam, Cold Harbor, Monocracy, Fredericksburg, Chancellorsville, and of course Gettysburg. They returned so often to Gettysburg they could quote from memory the inscriptions on most of the monuments.

They went in all seasons, driving over rolling farmlands. Rachel smoked her cigarettes, Essel his cigars, and the air inside the car became thick with co-mingled exhalations. The smoke intensified the crackling, acerbic intelligence between them. He remembered these drives as among the most aphrodisiacal times of their first amorous years. They stayed at small inns that advertised themselves as *Genuine Civil War*. After a full day of hiking over gray, green, empty battlefields, as their legs throbbed from long, slow exertion and their heads swam with the images of young soldiers falling tragically before their brothers, they could hardly contain themselves until they got back to the inn and hurtled themselves onto the noisy *Genuine Antique Civil War Bed* – or so such beds were advertised, as if, he now thought, it was an attraction to lie in a bed in which an artillery officer had bled to death.

Rachel gave up smoking after the stillborn, and eventually she got him to give up cigars. His abstinence lasted three years, during which they had the worse arguments of their long marriage. Nobody really won the cigar question. He went back to smoking occasionally, more or less on the sly, and she persisted in her disapproval.

A man, driving a station wagon filled with smoke, teenagers and cardboard file boxes containing 3-by-5 evidence cards on the debate proposition "Be it resolved: That The Environmental Protection Agency Should Be Given Full Regulatory Powers Over Industry," lost in his memories. The moronic, repetitive song on the radio had wormed its way into his head. As bad as the ice cream truck, he thought. "What is this *song* they keep playing?" Mr. Black complained. He heard the tired whine in his voice that he sometimes used with Rachel.

"Lowsparkahigheelboys," said Suzanne.

"Low *what*?" Mr. Black said, trying to laugh.

Suzanne enunciated slowly: "Low-Spark-Of-High-Heel-Boys."

Benjamin turned around in his seat and taunted her gently, "No-I'm-aluminuming-em-mum."

"That's real funny," Suzanne said with surprising venom. "Snappy patter."

Mike, who had yet to say much of anything, though there could be no doubt that that would change eventually, let out a strange yip, like a small dog. Essel tilted the mirror and glanced at Mike. Suddenly he realized what looked different about the boy. He'd parted his hair on the opposite side than usual. Essel spoke over his shoulder to Suzanne, "This music is terrible. It's just the same thing over and over."

"Mr. Black!" Suzanne patronized at the top of her voice, "with all due respect, o'leader or ours, you have *zero* taste in music."

"I can hear you, Miss Andersen, don't shout in my ear." He paused a beat. "What's the song about?"

"About?" Suzanne said incredulously. "Mr. Black, you don't need to know what it's about. It's about the low spark of high heel boys, what else? C'mon, Mr. Black, relax and get down on it." This last brought a quick round of affectionate laughs from members of both debate teams.

Essel glimpsed Benjamin watching Helen. The boy looked pleased with himself after his "aluminuming" joke and not at all stung by Suzanne's response. Then in the mirror he saw Helen exhale a short jet of smoke and return Benjamin's gaze with a deliberate look of her own, causing a flush to hurry to the boy's face.

*

The sunlight in San Diego was brighter, more intense, you might even say brittle, like it could splinter above your head. Essel had been coming to San Diego for a dozen years now, but he never failed to find himself pleasantly surprised with the beauty of the sky down here.

They arrived at the same building where Districts had always been held, Coleman Hall, and found it nearly deserted. They located the tournament board; first round match-ups were not posted yet. They were exceedingly early.

Suzanne took the lead. She'd heard about a coffee shop somewhere around the campus which was known for its Coca-Cola memorabilia. Could they go? Fine with Mr. Black; there was time. They could stow their evidence boxes in the corner of the coaches' lounge. He was going to stop in there anyway.

Minutes later they headed across campus, Suzanne leading the way, her blonde hair trailing like ribbons. Beside her was Mike, round-shouldered, taking long strides to stay in step. Suzanne abruptly veered off and approached two college students, boys standing under a tree, who were more than happy to give the pretty girl directions, which eventually led them to the coffee shop a block off campus, on

a street corner drenched in sunlight:
Jack's.

It looked like a Coca-Cola museum,
the kind of museum Essel remembered
coming upon in small towns along the
Chesapeake. Suzanne led them to a
booth. Mr. Black scooted in with the girls;
the boys sat opposite. On the table stood
an old-fashioned Coke bottle holding a silk
flower. The walls were covered with old-
fashioned Coke signs.

Easy Hospitality Serve Coca-Cola
Cool contrast to the summer sun
Drink Coca-Cola Good With Food

Essel recognized most of the signs
from long ago. Billboards and magazine
ads. Relics, he thought. There was one he
remembered as risqué. A bright-eyed girl
in a white two-piece bathing suit, sitting in
the sand, toes in the air. The sun bakes
the back of her shoulders. A petite blue
ribbon between her breasts draws your
eye. From outside the frame a man's arm
protrudes. He is holding a bottle of Coke
at a phallic tilt, offering it to her. Smack in
the middle of the ad is a single word:

Yes

"I saw a guy once," Mike addressed the others, leaning forward on his folded arms, "he had a necklace made out of pop tops. Nothing but pop tops. You couldn't believe it."

"I've seen those," said Suzanne, who tried to sound merry and bright but was showing signs of sluggishness. "They're all over."

Mike dropped his chin on his chest like Gregory Peck playing Atticus Finch and protested hard, "No, this one was really good. It was like a work of art."

"*These* are works of art," said Suzanne, nodding up at the signs.

Coke. It's a family affair.
"Coke Belongs"

Mike, plainly desperate to regain the attention, began reciting his Atticus Finch speech to himself. "Our courts have their faults, as does any human institution – "

"Knock it off, you kook," said Suzanne, punching his forearm.

" – our courts are the great levelers, and in our courts all men are created – "

"What are you, seized by some greater force?" said Suzanne. "You have this uncontrollable desire to rehearse *here and now*? You're not even giving that here."

So what was taking the waitress? thought Essel, though of course he knew it hadn't really been long. But he could sit there no longer. Forgodsakes it had only been a few minutes since last time. He leaned into Helen's shoulder and whispered, "Please order me a hamburger with french fries, if you will."

"I will, Mr. Black," said Helen.

Rachel would frown at the French fries, he thought as he scooted out.

"And a Coke?" asked Helen.

Essel looked down into her magnified eyes. "Absolutely, yes."

On his way he passed a large window that was lit blindingly from refracted sunlight. Near the door were two pinball machines, each with Coke motifs. He *did* like that girl, he thought as he pushed open the door.

Returning, Essel saw across the restaurant Suzanne chewing mischievously on a strand of hair. There were glasses of Coke on the table. He approached and saw by the boys' diverted eyes and Suzanne's ultra-attentive smile that something had happened. He scooted in and quickly surveyed the face of each of his debaters. It wasn't an argument. They were hiding something. Helen was sunk darkly into herself. Benjamin kept his glass in front of his face, sipping.

"Mike," said Mr. Black, "what are you people up to?"

Naturally Mike could be counted on to tattle. Suzanne scrunched her face, trying to shut him up, but the boy's young buck pride would not be stifled. "They just traded us," he said, both appalled and flattered.

"Don't believe him, Mr. Black," snapped Suzanne.

"I'm not lying," Mike said. He took on a mock gossip tone. "Helen had me and Suzanne had Benny and they just traded. Right in front of us. Like we weren't even sitting right here, looking right at them. Suzanne said – "

"You stop it, Mr. Jerkhead." Suzanne flicked at his mouth with her fingernails.

It could be a joke, thought Essel. A case of the girls teasing the boys. Benjamin's eyes were pained and expectant, focused on Mike. He didn't look embarrassed so much as worried that his friend was spoiling things with his immature big mouth. So, it was not a joke. The girls had each chosen a boy, made plans for him, and sometime this morning decided to change partners. Now they'd revealed their intentions to the boys and got them churned up.

Mr. Black wrapped his hands around his glass of Coke. If he showed his hands, he thought, they might see how serious he was. He looked from face to face. He decided that Helen was probably his best chance to head off this business. He met her big thick glasses and glared with intimidation. He was the adult here. He had authority here. He was to be obeyed. "There'd better not be *any* of that, Miss Rawson."

Helen was the best of the four at disguising her feelings, but she could not disguise in her "Yes, Mr. Black" that she was not persuaded by him. She looked over his shoulder and announced, "And here is our waitress with the food."

There was no waitress in sight. Mr. Black turned back around and gave Suzanne the same glare. Suzanne, dabbing her nose, hid behind her handkerchief.

A teenage boy and girl standing together excitedly, self-consciously, near a bed in a motel room.

"Don't worry, Mr. Black," said Suzanne. "We're just kidding around." She raised her glass to toast. "Here. Delicious and refreshing."

*

Essel had planned to attend at least one of the girls' debates. (The boys he would save the embarrassment.) He knew it was entirely possible that after today's two rounds both teams would be eliminated and they'd be on their way home first thing tomorrow morning.

He sat in the back of the classroom, out of the girls' line of sight. Besides himself, there were three other observers, and the judge, a graduate student. Essel began to feel a familiar sensation spread through him like a long swallow of Scotch. It was a kind of pre-nostalgia that he felt when he believed that he was witnessing the last time one of his own would debate.

The girls had drawn negative. They were up against a team from Morningside High with a good-to-excellent reputation: a short, pasty Buddha of a boy with brown acne, and his auburn-haired partner with tight, mod clothes and a candyness about him.

After the Buddha boy introduced the affirmative case, Suzanne, who now wore bright red lipstick that made the outline of her mouth flaming, mounted the standard negative argument that centered on *government interference*. It was the negative strategy that most teams used. Good teams often incorporated it into a multi-layered attack and delivered it with smug shorthand. Suzanne however was anything but smug. She sounded searching and tentative, like she was back at the start of the semester just learning the material. She gained some momentum near the end of her first negative, but mostly it was a tepid start for the girls.

Speaking second affirmative, the candy boy spent most of his time bolstering the affirmative's case and saved only the last minute to hammer dismissively at Suzanne's all-too-common arguments.

Then it was Helen's turn for second negative. Essel remembered that when Helen, as a freshman, first joined the forensics squad, he perceived it was because she was looking for a way to open up. Her self-absorbed manner and dark, cloaked appearance (including her thick glasses) probably gave other students the impression that Helen was bookish, though in fact she read books no more than the next B student. Bookish or not, she did not invite contact from others, and may even have repelled it without knowing. At fourteen, she may have sensed a need to find a way – now not later – of reaching beyond her own sullen and enclosed world. She lacked a way to communicate, so she aimed to find one by placing herself in tense formal circumstances wherein she would be required to make her thoughts clear to other people.

It did not come naturally to her. Instruction and advice seemed to go unheard. She chose to start off with the most difficult individual event, O.O. Her first speech, about her grandfather, was private and self-referential. After six tournaments of last place ballots (more than one judge found the speech "incomprehensible"), the naive look of failure on Helen's face was heartbreaking.

Essel, seeing her flounder and seeing that he was not getting through to her, asked Beverly Moskowitz to consider becoming a senior mentor to Helen. "You could help most by convincing her to form a debate team," he told Beverly with more than a pinch of exasperated irony.

Essel never learned what was said in the private huddles which took place that spring between Beverly and Helen, in the back of the classroom, in hallway corners at tournaments, but in the autumn, instead of dropping out of forensics as Essel expected, Helen returned and started a debate team with Suzanne, a virtual stranger to her. They never quite clicked into gear as a team. They liked each other, they grew to be friends, but Suzanne had too many other things in her life beyond forensics to give debate the serious attention it required, and Helen's attention, like Beverly Moskowitz before her, was most often focused on O.O., where she remained determined to succeed (and eventually did). She treated debate as if it were something of a necessary chore, performing it with casual skill. At tournaments Helen and Suzanne sometimes won a few rounds, but mostly lost as the competition got better. Essel still made occasional visits to the girls' rounds. Naturally he watched them closely through their ballots. But he had long ago given up hope of seeing in Helen a trace of Beverly's native genius for debate.

So what was this in the first round of Districts? Helen, second negative, threw up a powerfully reasoned attack spiked with derision. Her countenance was smooth as glass, jabbing the air with evidence cards, and her counter-arguments were sharp as glass, quoting Jefferson from memory at length and with biting accuracy. She attacked with ruin, opening gaping fallacies in the affirmative's case, ridiculing analogies, mutilating their logic, all the while fixing her enormous eyes on the judge, challenging him to disagree.

Essel's brow glistened with the sweat of astonishment.

The boys of the affirmative were tossed into a bewildered scramble. They huddled and whispered in confusion at each other. Like a good team, they were trying not to panic. In his rebuttal the Buddha boy set about repairing the damage. A frantic edge entered his manner as he ignored Suzanne's arguments entirely and concentrated on Helen's brutal second negative. This was a dubious if inevitable strategy. As one affirmative argument after another fell flat and the realization overtook him that the affirmative's case was decimated, he hunched into a rounded Buddha slump. In the end his voice failed to conceal his boyish hatred for Helen personally.

Suzanne, suddenly alert and confident, scored in her rebuttal by returning to her own best negative arguments, then going on to repeat, however less forcefully, some of Helen's attacks.

Standing for the affirmative's final rebuttal, the candy boy approached the front with a mock stagger. It was something Mike might have done. A clot of phlegm thickened his voice as he began to speak.

Essel retrieved his copy of the tournament brackets from his briefcase and scanned Helen and Suzanne's bracket.

Considering this kind of overpowering strength displayed by Helen, it was conceivable they could beat any team who stood before them and the quarter-finals. Were Beverly Moskowitz sitting next to her, Helen would be looking at a trip to the State Championships.

Helen rose to conclude the debate. She chose her words deliberately, her lips a tight smile. Her opponents had sidestepped this argument and that, she pointed out. Errors of omission in their own affirmative case were by themselves enough to cost them the debate, "When have we heard such shoddy reasoning?" she asked the judge, but then they'd also failed to respond to the negative on the following points... And in the end: *Reductio ad absurdum*. The proposition is overthrown." She turned and faced full to the affirmative team's table. Let them get a good look at her.

A dark-haired teenager, her profile splendid and womanly, her chin up, a tall girl but not stooped-shouldered from trying to look shorter, facing her defeated opponents. The Buddha boy would not look up from his flowsheet. The candy boy pretended to be busy refiling evidence cards. Helen, having gutted her opponents, added, "Swiss cheese, gentleman. Your case." The judge smirked involuntarily through his nostrils before he could catch himself. Helen thanked the judge and sat down.

Essel left the room. Soon he would go to their designated meeting place in the cafeteria where he'd find Mike, drained nearly to unconsciousness from a hysterical outburst in a losing cause; and Benjamin, his face drained, his pale blue shirt spotted with sweat. Soon, when the girls arrived he would tell them with tempered assurance that he thought they probably took that one but not to get excited and lose their concentration. "You got lucky this time," he would tell them. "You drew a team that wasn't prepared for Districts."

That would be soon. First there was the Men's room; first there was his racing heart.

*

The motel was only two blocks off campus, an old two-story, yellowing stucco. Essel's room smelled of disinfectant. He had seen to it with the clerk at the desk that his room was between those of his two debate teams.

He visited the bathroom first, then set out his things. While at it he retrieved the half-pint and set it on the dresser.

Once he was organized away he stepped out on the portico and went looking for an ice machine. He found one around the corner, but it wasn't working. He came back to his room and poured two fingers in a flimsy plastic cup and added a splash of tap water. He took a seat on the edge of the bed and lit the Churchill. A print of a forest stream was secured to the wall. He thought about going next door and giving the boys a good-effort speech.

After the end of the second round they'd met for an early supper at the cafeteria in the basement of Coleman Hall. The boys sat there smoldering and humiliated. They had every right to be, as Essel knew. He'd read their ballots, which he was keeping until he thought about what to do with them. Both rounds were brutal. Mike muttered self-consolingly that he thought the second debate was close. Benjamin agreed without conviction.

Essel drew on the Churchill and decided a pep talk could wait. Instead he decided to call home with the good news about the girls.

"How exciting for them," said Rachel, who was in the middle of cleaning up after making herself an early supper.

"If it goes tomorrow as I suspect," said Essel, "that will put us back home sometime after dark. Or later – " he paused a moment to consider just what that would mean, "but I'll call if we're going to be late." Then after another pause: "She *was* good. She truly was good. I could shake her for the time she wasted."

"That's not what you really think."

"No."

There was a long pause. To Rachel it was unmistakable: he was drawing on a cigar. She could read every fluctuation in the rhythm of their conversation. "Are you smoking?" She made it sound more like a question than a reprimand.

But this time she was slightly mistaken. Essel had paused not to draw on the Churchill, but because he had heard coming from the boys' side through the membrane-thin wall a phone ring.

Rachel could not resist some ribbing. "Did you put them in the glove compartment last night?" she said.

"Please don't start tonight," he said.

Rachel didn't want to darken his hour of triumph. She knew he would douse his adrenaline with Scotch, smoke his victory cigar, read in the room's most comfortable spot until he grew drowsy, and go to bed with the past – and this newest pride – bundled at his breast. "I'm sorry to hear about the boys," she said.

And just as she could tell Essel's every nuance by listening, he in turn knew that as they spoke Rachel was sponging the sink counter and scraping specks of food with her thumbnail from the strip of caulking between the tiles. He knew the last thing she'd do before leaving the kitchen would be to wipe the taps clean of water spots. He knew exactly how long each action took, in what direction she moved, the look on her face. He knew all the domestic minutia there was to know about her. At times this knowledge was the most important in his life. But right now, as he listened to her talk about her day filled with chores and people who were amusingly familiar to them both, he was too distracted to listen. He heard the girls' door open, and Suzanne's careful footsteps sound on the concrete portico as she went past his window, and the door close, and Helen following. There was a brittle knock on the boys' door. He had to get off the phone. He pretended to be too bushed to keep talking.

Sitting on the foot of the bed, a glass ashtray beside him, Essel sipped his drink and listened. With the four of them together, what could happen that was really so bad? A little smooching? Maybe they'd all go out on a double date. To Jack's. What was so wrong with that? He heard Suzanne's high laugh, and Benjamin's maturing baritone. He remembered that Benjamin joined forensics in the first place because teachers and students kept telling him he had a good voice. What a reason. There was a loud *thump* on wood, followed by Mike's comic "Ow!" Suzanne let out a shrieking laugh, and Helen shushed her soundly. Essel looked around the room. Surely all these rooms were identical. There it was: Mike had bumped his head on the headboard. "Mr. Jerkhead," Suzanne said at the top of her voice. Essel turned on the television.

He poured himself a second drink. Then he saw shadows against the curtains but couldn't tell whose. The door to the girls' room opened and closed. He quickly got up and turned off the television. He sat and listened. Now who was in which room? It was quiet for several minutes, then there was sneezing in the boys room. It was Mike. Huge, rapid sneezes, six in a row and more, and after a pause a few more. Essel remembered once reading that the response by some adolescent boys to arousal was often a short fit of sneezing, perhaps reacting to a sudden change of temperature or shifting of blood. He remembered that when he read this, besides thinking how odd it sounded, and foreign to his own experience, he immediately thought of Mike, a habitual masturbator if ever he saw one.

Suddenly Essel felt ridiculous, like he was caught in the middle of a bad comedy. Then he heard water running in the boys' bathroom and he could not stop himself. He had to know. He put his ear against the cold bathroom wall. He heard Suzanne humming. He listened. It was that awful song from the car, moronic and repetitive, on and on. High spark or something like that. He shoved himself away from the wall and glared with distress the other way.

You must understand there was no way Essel Black could have known what happened next. But you must also understand that he knew what was happening then and there as surely as if he were standing in the dark room with them, watching as Helen removed her big round glasses with small ceremony and set them on the bedside table. He knew that Helen got in bed first and saved the last of her clothing to be removed under the covers. He knew that Benjamin sat on the edge of the bed still wearing his shoes, wishing she had helped him, if only unbuttoning his shirt, but then undressing with the swiftness of stripping for gym and removing everything but his shorts and easing uncertainly into bed, folding one arm around her, his palm on her back. He knew that Helen led the way, decided the passion of their kissing, the timing of their nakedness, the arrangement of their bodies. He knew that ultimately that arrangement would have Benjamin stretched full on top of her, her cheek on the pillow and her eyes turned from his until the moment he entered. In his mind's eye, Essel Black watched as he sipped his Scotch. He saw that no words passed between them.

And while he could not have known, he *did* know that in the other room no such thing happened. Perhaps there was smooching and groping. Suzanne displayed her flirtatious charm and Mike put on his goofball antics, but there was no more than that.

A man alone smoking a cigar in a dark motel room. He couldn't remember when he'd last had two cigars in one day. Heat sores had begun to form inside his lower lip. Nausea was gathering in the back of his throat. Now he did something he hated doing and almost never did. He snubbed out the Churchill, with no small feeling of waste. Now a vague after-supper discomfort he'd been feeling suddenly sharpened into a stuttering pain in his left armpit and down his arm to the top of his wrist. There was a tingling in the side of his neck, an itchy numbness. His breathing was coming harder. A rising tide of vertigo made him shake his head. Angina twinge, he thought. He laid on his back, the bed giving way with a slow creak beneath his weight, and thus he remained, eyes open wide, waiting for it to pass.

*

Next day Benjamin attended the girls' first round. Mike, having bounced back from yesterday's batterings and full of energy, took off, he said, "to explore the campus." Essel remained in the coaches' lounge. He felt blurred around the periphery. He thought it would be better if he just sat it out. After the first round he got himself up off the couch and went to the cafeteria to sit around a table with the girls (and Benjamin) and wait for the decisions to be posted.

"We ran into trouble this time," Suzanne said, stating a fact.

"I don't know," Benjamin added quickly. He was wearing his same pale blue shirt, which was wrinkled. No tie. "I thought you won. Easily. Helen? You two were good."

But Helen was sunken into herself. She ignored Benjamin.

"Affirmative just isn't our game," Suzanne announced.

Essel surmised that Helen had not debated today as she had yesterday. The ballot which he later read in the coaches' lounge would confirm this. He sensed that the girls were headed for another poor round and just like that would be eliminated.

Benjamin nudged his chair flush against Helen's. The boy had been trying to fawn over her all morning. During the walk over to Coleman Hall and all during breakfast, he made attempts to touch her arm or whisper support and witticisms in her ear or steal looks at her when he thought his coach Mr. Black wasn't watching. Helen fended him off by sinking deeper into herself. Now he was at it again. Helen lit a cigarette in irritation.

Then as if suddenly struck by the idea, Helen retrieved her tablet of flowsheets which was propped against her briefcase on the floor and with an obvious show of disdain plopped it down before her. The top page was obliterated with scribbled words and lines from the debate. She tore off a large scrap from the second page and started writing on it in careful, right-leaning script. It was a letter, not entirely on display for everyone to read but not purposely shielded either.

Dearest,

Essel wondered if this was her low-rider boyfriend. Or was the letter just for show? He refused to read it though it lay right before his eyes. Helen stopped writing after a couple of sentences, once it became apparent that Benjamin had a chance to see. Then suddenly turning surreptitious, she slipped the scrap between the pages of the tablet.

The drive home was smokeless and cheerless except for a smattering of mindless chatter from Suzanne and Mike. They made a pit stop in Oceanside. Some things Essel simply preferred not to think about. Watching Benjamin fighting off the onrush of first heartache, Essel told himself the boy would get over it. He saw Helen sunken darkly into herself, wrestling with a confusion she had not anticipated. It was sad, he thought, that over and over he should observe his students maturing and feel both glad and repelled. His own death was coming. On this subject Essel had never wanted to keep 3-by-5 cards.

Nor did he prefer to think about how he would hide last night from Rachel. She saw sadness in him as surely as she smelled cigar smoke on his clothing. And she would know immediately that losing at a tournament was not the cause. She would press for details, and the details would unlatch a trunk of memories long ago locked by mutual silent agreement.

They arrived back at school shortly after three. There was some fast stowing of evidence boxes in the classroom. Out in the hallway under the awning the four debaters bid one another perfunctory good-byes. Suzanne asked if anyone wanted a ride home. Mike said yes.

"I'm not riding in that thing," Helen joked weakly. Suzanne hugged her around the waist then took off for the parking lot, with Mike in tow.

Helen wouldn't look at Benjamin. She nodded good-bye quickly to Mr. Black and walked away, headed across campus, carrying her black bag over her shoulder.

Benjamin pretended not to be watching her. "Thanks for taking us, Mr. Black. Next year we'll give'm a better run, ok?" It sounded like something the boy felt obligated to say, as a member of next year's first-ranked debate team.

Essel searched for something to say that would shudder down the boy's spine. "You lost badly."

"I know."

"No you don't. You don't know how badly."

"I do. I was there."

"Then either you don't care enough, or you have too much resilience for your own good. Both of you."

"Not me. I'll go home and agonize. Mike's the one gets over it fast. It's just a debate to him. Maybe it meant more, you know, being Districts and everything, but really it was about the same to him."

"But *you* agonize."

"Yes, sir," said Benjamin, flustered beneath his coach's glare. "I admit I don't much like this proposition, but the debate means a lot to me. It eats at me to lose."

Essel wondered how he would survive watching the succession of losses that Benjamin and Mike would suffer beginning in the autumn, matched against first-ranked teams at every tournament. "You better be prepared to lose a lot next year," he said, and for an instant he thought maybe if he just took the boy by the shoulders and shook hard enough he could shake him out of his mediocrity.

But now Benjamin was anxious to go. "Lookit, I'll see you Monday, Mr. Black." The boy turned and started in Helen's direction, following what he must have thought was a discrete distance behind, as if Helen would be unaware of him following.

OUR MISTAKE

First, a little something about Jack Silverstern – weeknight announcer, man of ace high chops, Jazz King of this ACC metropolis, my employee and friend. Jack's knowledge of Jazz (and it was *knowledge*, not the mere familiarity I've seen over the years in many a needle- and now laser-dropper) reached far back beyond the Dixielanders, to the very root rhythms, and seeped into the smallest hairline cracks of improvised musical sound. While he would never flaunt it, for he was a gentleman to his friends in accordance with his native Chicagoan tradition, Jack was also a huge Sinatra scholar, a savant of major American sports, and a hepcat for the special curvatures of pussy. His ON-AIR presence was Dewar's; his cool was glib-tongued and white enough to maintain a sufficient percent of our *ATC* audience, yet so well informed with arcane patterns of black speech that he garnered – are you ready? – a 38 share in selected ZIPs.

Check out this sample riff I saved off my skimmer: "With 'Phoebe's Samba' that's...[smooth pause]...Ralph Moore from his album *Furthermore*, Ralph Moore on tenor, Roy Hargrove on trumpet, Benny Green piano, Peter Washington bass, and Victor Lewis on drums. Get...sent. Two minutes before ten, Jack Silverstern with you. I ain talkin' no stuff when I say I don't think you really want to go for a walk this evening. If the dog wants to go for a walk, you just open the door and tell'em, 'Dog, you jivey, walk yourself.' Fair and cold tonight, with lows in the mid to upper *twenties*. Spring is, hey, around the corner, but ain't in the backyard yet."

Over the years, many listeners have expressed to me their surprise, even bewilderment, upon learning that Jack, regardless of the contradiction his Hebraic surname presented, was not African-American. Those of us in management liked it that way and limited his personal appearances.

Though, another reason also drove this decision to keep Jack out of the public eye. Jack was prototypic radio. For all his ON-AIR cool, he was disturbing to look at with too much sober scrutiny. Not that Jack didn't know plenty about dressing cool and conducting himself in a manner befitting coolness. But staring you in the face were those distended nostrils, and a whiny complexion pitted with teenage acne scars deep enough to spackle with a trowel. As a tip o' the hat to beboppers of old, Jack applied a pinch of wax to his big black moustache, but the effect was as if he hadn't bothered to clean up after eating one of the enormous greasy subs from Nick's Deli, which he kept within arm's reach during his shift. But more – his lips, though mostly hidden by the moustache, were reptilian, his body seemed to be rising to its own level like water, his dark eyes had the general shape and attention span of a seagull's, and his fingertips were stained from years of nonfilter cigarettes.

Yeah, well, I'm hardly beautiful myself, but Jack's repellent appearance is important to note because, to his credit, he refused to allow it to dampen his tinderbox flirtations.

Nothing contributed more to the Silverstern persona around the station than Jack's many fabled stories of "successful negotiations" in dark, smoky bars, and "doin' the triple-X do" in dark, sweaty bedrooms. Jack's women were a perfumed breed both mysterious and unnerving to we whiteboys gathered in the library, listening with wistful ears.

"They're not whores outright," said Jack, whose given name was Ronald J. Silverstern, but sometime in his Windy City youth he chose Jack as the coolest of possibilities. "They're classy ladies in their own right. Put it like this. Say one, let's pick at random – Ceci – say Ceci is out on a party night and it's been stone, I mean *stone*. She came dressed for bear and found the woods empty. All right, now she's in the cab for home. So it's not *inconceivable* that for the adventure of the thing, Ceci is going to offer to pay her fare by inviting the cabby to shilly shally on into the back with her. Just a few minutes. Long enough so this sweet and lonely – not to say horny – little lady will feel not so down." Ceci, it turned out, worked for an escort service, but that was not how Jack met her. Jack did not purchase his women.

A favorite grabber of Jack's was a quick line about a drunken man in the heat of passion inserting his tongue into a woman's anus. Jack didn't say it was a favorite trick of his own, but he left no doubt that he had sampled this particular delicacy enough times to speak of it with familiarity, no, with *knowledge*.

Maybe none of it was true. Maybe Jack's greatest talent – greater even than his supreme ON-AIR presence – was creative lying. But now and then I did see women on his arm who might fit this description. Besides, each evening as Jack arrived at work trailing clouds of hipness, he made us believe, so I take it as the truth without undue exaggeration.

If, as wise men say, at the heart of us all there lies an animal of one kind or another, then Jack – Jazz King and overheated Cub fan – was, in the Chaucerian sense, *a moost happy pigge.*

So you can understand our amazement.

Her name is Delphine Potocka. Unusual name isn't it. Sort of Polish or Slavic or Eastern Europe, at least. Maybe I should say it's an unusual name for a Denver girl who comes from English-French stock and a broken marriage. Three months removed from taking an undergraduate degree in economics from one of the region's high-brow colleges (whose name promulgates a pair of Anglo-Saxon monarchs), Delphine came to me. She had aesthetically pale skin and pearly black hair that she wore in a classic co-ed style. Her eyes were small and pale brown, and so guileless and disarming I could hardly look at her steadily – *me*, who not many years ago was twice her age. There was a slight floral scent about her, and she seemingly had no intention or willingness to sleep with the program director. She was alert, smart, taciturn, and I hired her as an assistant. We strolled together through the station and I introduced her to whomever didn't appear too busy to interrupt. Then I shook her delicate hand and said I looked forward to seeing her bright and early Monday morning.

That evening, working late – conventional wisdom has it that a good program director is one who eats and breathes radio – I looked up from the spread of data on my desk to see Jack in my doorway.

He was sporting a fancy new fedora in the Francis
Albert fashion, smoking a Camel shorty. My door, I
am not too modest to say, is always open, though Jack
rarely came through it all the way, preferring instead
a more casual, less power-structured stance between
the jambs.

"So Boss," said Jack. "Tell me about the new
recruit." He'd been in the building hardly thirty
seconds.

"She's not for you," I said with all the
indifference I could muster.

"I hear otherwise."

"You hear wrong."

"You're not keeping her for yourself?"

"No. Ms. Delphine Potocka apparently did not
seek the position in hopes of getting laid."

"That's what they all say."

"Sad to say, I think this time it's true. She's
pleasant enough to look at, but there's more to it."

"What's wrong with her?"

She may have suffered a bad case of
seriousness as a child. It's left its scars."

"Is that all. Well, Boss, you know what they
say in Jamaica."

"What do they say in Jamaica?"

"The good cock he crows in any henhouse."

And so on like that. Jack and I did not
converse so much as banter. I like to think that I'll do
whatever it takes to communicate with my people.
That's what it took with Jack. He placed a higher
value on street smarts than school smarts. Jack had
skipped college. He didn't like what it did to people.
Those he knew who'd gone to college came out with

zero capacity to function on the street. He may also have intuitively known that when sometime during college he was asked to direct his eyes to the page for long periods of time, he'd find this not suited to his temperament.

"Boss," Jack continued, "I just want to say, on behalf of the troops, thanks for keeping us so well fed. Bravo Zulu."

This remark, loaded with history, was partly I think in reference to my open-handed practice of sharing our good fund-raising fortune with ON-AIR personnel whenever I happened to have a little extra corporate green left in my budget, and partly in reference to my hiring practices per assistants, which over the years betrayed a strain favoring young, pretty women, some of whom, depending on their preferences – Classical, Jazz, News – found their way into the arms of one or another of our boss jocks.

Jack recognized upon first swoop that Delphine was never going to allow herself to be tongued on all fours, not even by the man she loved, whoever that would to be. He discovered, as did I, that Delphine could fend for herself in ways learned from her scorned mother. Jack was even compelled to do a quick diagnostic search for signs of lesbianism. She rented a house with her three college roommates. They had all been pretty girls on campus, but only three were still pretty. The fourth, Molly, was drinking, getting fat, and sleeping around. "I suppose it's not a fatal combination," Delphine said to Jack, "but it's taking away her looks."

"Delphine's no lesbian," Jack ultimately announced to me after concluding his examination.

He was standing in my doorway late one night, as back in the studio some long baritone sax track was playing. "I say she's a virgin in all but the strictest technical sense," said Jack. I agreed.

Not to put too fine a point on it, soon after Jack began coming by the station each day around noon, which couldn't have been long after he woke up, ostensibly to "do a little work in the library," then accompanying Delphine to Nick's Deli two blocks down from the station; and soon after Jack and Delphine began sitting together after work at the hammered tin bar of one of his choice establishments of libation; and after attending Jazz clubs and college basketball games together; and after offering to the rest of us their mutual thoughts on movies – that is, soon after it became too late to avert their eyes from one another, Delphine fell strangely ill, lost energy, began to lose weight frighteningly fast, went through a series of macabre tests, and was diagnosed with leukemia.

*

You're giving an awful picture of Jack. What's this? Italics. I see. I am to be italicized. It figures. To remove everything I say one step, so it will mean less. But if you're going to describe Jack you might as well do it right. You're only talking about one small side of him, the public Jack, or the sophisticated Jack. You superficial bastard. Sure, Jack wasn't attractive in the conventional way, but that was one of the wonderful things about him. I didn't even think of him romantically at first. Not my type. And what should I care what he looked like? You saw what I looked like, for godsakes. And I got to like his smoky smell. I liked that he talked smart and could take charge of a situation. He had a good time, but I never saw him stinking drunk. I liked the fact that he carried a lot of cash and could wear an expensive hat convincingly. And you make a big deal about the marks on his face, but I think they gave his face character. That's Jack – character, something you can't fully appreciate. I don't doubt he said and did all those smarmy things. I saw evidence enough. That was another part of the "cool" Jack. That's not what counts in the long run, is it? I would never have fallen in love with the person you describe. You're forgetting, or maybe you don't know, how Jack could be when he wasn't trying to be Frank Sinatra. He was very warm. He was very loyal. He took care of me without smothering me.

*

Thus, chastened by my assistant – linked to me via the Compaq at her desk – I'll continue by offering the confession (I might as well say it now) that Delphine and I did, once, shortly after her initial employment, engage in friendly (or so I thought) fornication, one rainy night at my house. Delphine has ever since referred to the delightful things we did to one another that night only very privately, only very sparingly, and only as "our mistake."

Delphine began chemotherapy. At first, she kept most of the effects of it from view; some she couldn't. She continued to lose weight, but at a markedly decelerated rate. Her pale skin took on a

waxy sheen as if cold to the touch, and her brown
eyes lost much of their luminosity. She took off
Fridays and no longer stayed late to finish work,
though I will say that while at work she maintained a
strict attention to detail which might be described as
compulsive. I think the work held her together in
some ways.

But there was, of course, much more going on
besides what was visible to me. Every weekend
Delphine went through a two-day post-radiation
ordeal of constant nausea, vomiting, and dry heaves.
There were barbiturate suppositories, platelet
transfusions, and clotted blood extracted every few
days from her ear canals. The taciturn Ms. Potocka
would expend the last of her energy by throwing
harrowing and obscene tantrums. She threw them at
Jack, at her roommates (who tried to stay clear), and
even at her mother, who was now on the scene,
having quit her job and moved out from Denver to
join her daughter.

These are terrible things to speak of. You may
call me a misogynist, but the fact is I say them
because they are no more than true. I heard them from
Jack, who remained at her side every waking hour he
was not ON-AIR. It's not that in communicating these
things to us Jack relished the details. He issued them
in dribs and drabs, and with an air – not to read more
into it than there was – an air of penance. To watch
your beloved go through such horrors. How awful.

Then after five or six weeks of chemo, the
effects began to show in Delphine with shocking
drama. As she had been told would happen, her hair
was drained of it pearly beauty, then fell out, leaving

grayish tufts which for reasons unclear she chose not to conceal. Jack bought her a sharp black beret, but she wore it only when outside in the cold. Her skin became translucent as a baby's temple, as if it would puncture from the slightest prick of a pencil. She virtually lost the power of movement, getting up from her desk only when there was simply no way to avoid it. I reassigned her tape traffic duties to my other, more high-pitched assistant, Linda, and redoubled Delphine's PSA and ticket-giveaway work, thereby allowing her to spend almost all her day at her desk, though there was a lot of phone work which I know can be exhausting.

What happened to Jack during this time was hardly less dramatic. Here was his first close look at death. His eyes recoiled in a stare. His heavy smoking became an unbroken chain. He had stumbled upon a lodestone of some universal fear and wasn't sure yet how to react. When he was up and full of energy, he seemed to pride himself in having done the manly thing, risen to the occasion as Nietzsche says. He was giving help and comfort to his love when she most needed it. But when he was down, he got whiny and mean.

"Why do I get this PSA?" Jack complained to me from my doorway one night. "This doesn't belong on my show."

"What's wrong with it?" I said, taking it from him. "The Red Cross?"

"It has no place on a Jazz show," he said, stepping back into the doorway and dragging on a freshly lit Camel. "Put it on during *Morning Edition* or something. I can't come out of Clifford Brown and start in asking people for blood."

"It's a public service."

"Look at this." He stepped fully into the office, leaned over the desk, pressed his finger onto the page and read from the PSA. "'Particular call for special blood types now urgently needed in the African-American community.' What's that about? *My* audience is going to know. It says please give blood to the niggers out there shooting each other."

"Soften it," I said. "Put it in your own words."

"How 'bout I jis don't say it at all," Jack said, and went back to the studio without the copy.

When in the library, wedged between the narrow shelves of CDs, among us guys, Jack still told stories lewd and lusty about the past, but now these stories, all of which we'd heard before, took on a malicious twist, almost sadistic. I hardly have to add that none of the stories were about Delphine. Our collective speculation concluded that while Jack and Delphine had probably at one time entered into sexual congress, they certainly did not now, which meant, incredibly, that Jack Silverstern was living a celibate life. I understand that Jack and Delphine's mother became fond of one other, except for her disapproval of his smoking in the house.

The one thing that did not change in Jack was, not surprisingly, his ON-AIR work. I offer as evidence another cut from my skimmer: "From the Jobim album, that was Frank... [smooth pause] ...and Claus Ogerman's arrangement of the classic Irving Berlin tune, 'Change Partners.' And speaking of classics, those of you who catch our Classical show in the daylight hours, I gotta tell you about something I overheard in the record store t'other day. I'm standing in line see and I hear a lady in front of me ask for an album with Frank Sinatra and Itzhak Perlman, the violinist. Now I'm thinking, what? Frank never did no album with Itzhak Perlman, though if they ever did do an album I'd bet it'd be one hell of an album. Turns out, the lady was listening to the radio and what she heard was the Violin Sonata of Cesar Franck, played by Itzhak Perlman, so I guess it was announced as the Franck Sonata."

And this while his own lady was dying. The man remained a pro.

*

You still haven't got it, have you? Isn't that what they used to say in est? 'I got it!' I'll bet you were in est, though you'll probably deny it. You're very good at denying things. You never bothered to ask but let me spell a few things out for you. Imagine that your body turns traitor on you. I always used to think that my body and my real self – the one inside – were united, connected together. So what happens when the two turn out to be just thrown together by chance, and you find out that one doesn't really have anything to do with the other? Sure, Jack got scared. I got ugly right before his eyes, not just on the outside, either. As you say, I threw harrowing and obscene tantrums. That's very generous of you. Let me say it. I looked hideous from this disease. (Such a nasty word.) So what? Isn't that the test you give every news story to determine its worth? So what?

Voyeurs   DJB

*The fact is, Jack did stay with me, and he gave me
what I needed most. He listened. He would sit in my
bedroom all weekend, or in the living room or out on
the porch and just listen to me talk. Even when he got
extremely tired he would light another cigarette and
keep listening. I'm sure it wouldn't occur to you that I
had a lot of things to say then. Why am I defending
myself to you? I don't need this. As if there's not
enough else to worry about, feeding the cat, getting to
work on time – because we wouldn't want to be late
for work, would we? You. I could tell from the minute
I met you that you would be trouble, that you would
have the right words and the right touch at the right
time. I'm sure it's not overt, really. It's just your way.
Well, there's nothing I can do about our mistake. So
fine, go on with your lies.*

*

I recall that during the time my assistant was
in the throes of her therapy she was scheduled to take
a three-day computer class, gratis from the station,
because I wanted to give her a hand. Her illness
prevented her from attending, but, as you can see, it
did not prevent her from nonetheless gaining a firm
grasp on our computer network.

Eventually there came a time for Delphine
when the news began to turn positive, one chip of
good news after another. She was not out of danger
yet by any means, but her appearance became less
haunted and fateful in the Schubertian sense, and she
was clearly going in the right direction. Her birthday
was approaching. Jack informed us there would be a

surprise party. He didn't say whose inspiration this was. He seemed not to have been the one, but he was also a willing participant, not just the messenger of the event.

It came off well. A large group of us – staff members and some of Delphine's old school chums – waited quite a while in the dark of Delphine's living room, drinking, before Jack and Delphine returned home from dinner on the town. Then, Delphine was surprised. A picture taken by her mother at the moment of impact – SURPRISE! – was later framed and presented to the couple. Delphine keeps it on her desk. It shows her stepping through the inner door, her face tilted upward, her eyes closed in delight, her perfect upper teeth displayed in a wide, open-mouthed, honest smile. Her hair has begun to grow in, and she's wearing it brushed back with authority. Immediately back of her in the small vestibule is Jack in overcoat and smartly tied scarf. One eye is squinting from the flash, the other, protected by the bent brim of his hat, is on Delphine. He is wearing one of the finest Silverstern grins. On his arm is a white box of long stem flowers, tied with white ribbon.

All surprise parties are just parties with ten minutes of surprise tacked onto the front. Once everyone confirmed to one another that Delphine had indeed been surprised, we got on with the party as usual. Everyone was a drink or two ahead of Jack and Delphine, but they made fast to catch up. Jack had his Scotch and Camel. Delphine was so buoyed by the friends around her I doubt that alcohol could have made her the slightest bit gladder, but she kept a

White Russian in her hand always, perhaps to keep her roommate Molly company.

As the party moved along, I found myself in the kitchen and I eased into a cluster around Delphine that included – what a jackpot – all three roommates. Delphine had changed out of her black evening dress with its swanky low-cut back, into a black turtleneck. Up close under the bright kitchen light it was apparent just how much healthier Delphine had become. Next to her two pretty roommates (the sort of ladies I would gladly hire if they came to me with a passable resume), Delphine still showed pale signs of illness. But standing with Molly, well, one of the refrains sung by many throughout the evening was "Delphine looks better than Molly."

Over the next half-hour I nudged closer to Delphine until finally I was close enough to whisper in her ear. She appeared to be very pleased that I had come, and I reciprocated with looks of genuine warmth and many words of good wishes in light of the terrible time she had faced, was still facing, was apparently coming through. "I admire you for standing up like you have," I said slowly, my eyes stinging from vodka and dammed up tears. I realized even then that I probably had no business saying any such thing, given the generally oblivious attitude I had adopted ever since her illness was first announced. But my words were heartfelt. She kissed me on the cheek, and we were friends at that instant.

Having offered my intimate comment for the night, I leaned back only to discover that Molly had been peering into our whispered conversation. The three of us were standing so close we could have been fibers in a rug. Molly, a chunky girl, about an inch over five feet, with fashionably spiked glossy-black hair, was deep in her cups. I got the impression that she drank as a means of fighting off the slowly dawning realization that she was well on her way toward a catastrophic failure as a woman. I can recognize such things. Molly was giving Delphine and me a sisterhood scrutiny, with the glazed tunnel vision that alcohol confers to the eyes of intense young drunks.

Delphine noticed Molly's eavesdropping and my displeasure at Molly's eavesdropping. Always one to deflect praise toward others, she responded to my heartfelt words with some self-effacing crap about not being able to have survived without the help of her loyal friends, including Molly, and of course Jack.

At this last, Molly was compelled to blurt, "Jack. Watch it, Delphie." She was all balloon tongue and diphthongs. "Jack'll leave you the second he sees a pretty face – correct that – a pretty *ass* pass his way."

I took this as a drunken stab at humor and chuckled into my vodka for the sake of the situation, feeling my feet sinking as if in soft fresh bread. Delphine laughed, too, showing disdain for the seeming inevitable.

*

Great. Let's kick Molly while she's down while we're at it. She'd love hearing this. If a guy starts drinking and sleeping around, it's almost honorable, to get some sleaze in his life while he's still young.

*Some men devote their lives to it, and Jack had a
pretty strong taste of it himself, but they don't become
catastrophic failures as men. Later on it's just
something that matured you in ways you hadn't
planned on. Don't worry about Molly. She can take
care of herself. As for what happened at the party, if
you want the truth, I did think at the time that Jack
would leave, eventually. Molly got that idea from me.
She was just repeating it as a sort of clumsy empathy.
Jack had asked me to move in with him, now that I
was over the worst of it. But I'd decided, without my
mother's influence I might add, to stay where I was. I
still needed to see.*

*

Yeah, right. A sturdy revelation, that. Since
she brought up the subject, allow me to speak a
moment of Delphine's mother. As is apparent upon
meeting her, she married and gave birth to her only
child at a young age, indeed, about the time her
girlfriends were just discovering the steamy
underbelly of drive-in movies. It is likewise apparent
upon observing mother and daughter side by side and
comparing their utterances re:men that the Potocka
divorce a decade ago must have been unspeakably
brutal. That's all I'll say on the matter, lacking
specifics.

Anyway, it was at this same surprise party that
I finally managed to bring a key member of the
management team on-line for my coup. I had been
quietly building a data base of ammunition for several
weeks. My plan, as I laid out to our marketing

director Caitlin Boss, was to bolster our numbers among white affluents by expanding the NPR talk programming late into the night. I was aiming for midnight, but I knew I would settle for eleven. This would in effect squeeze Jazz out of the schedule. I considered it the necessary price of success.

These things I said to Caitlin Boss, who sat with me snugly at the top of the stairs where we could see fellow partiers well before they came within earshot of our conversation. Caitlin Boss is a moxied careerist infused with an attitude of personal control and a trust in numbers. I dislike her intensely. Seeking to convince her, I reasoned that while it was true that Jack's, rather, Jazz's audience was good in terms of AQH, it did poorly during fund raisers. She knew even better than I that Jazz was our low card in regard to money. "Jazz is high in the wrong sections of our ADI," I said. "Our audience is the NPR audience. Look at the numbers for *Morning Edition* and *ATC.* Why not serve *our* audience? Why turn them away every night at seven? Why not play to our fullest potential?"

I was not telling Caitlin Boss anything new. She could have formulated my plan herself. When versions of it had come up during past lunchroom conversations, Caitlin Boss always smiled at the thought of upping our cume a projected 15,000 but balked at cutting Jazz. That was too severe for her. She didn't see how we could do it without suffering damage to our image in the community. Besides, Caitlin Boss, like the rest of us, considered Jack to be part of our radio family. But perhaps tonight the purr of booze and good vibes made my reasoning sound softer on her ears, for we were soon nodding in cruel and co-operative harmony, a pair of team players willing to make the hard calls.

"I know how this affects Jack," I empathized. "I don't want you to think I'm overlooking that. But ultimately, our fondness for Jack gets placed in its proper perspective. It becomes part of the structure of the decision. You can see how important or unimportant a piece it is."

It seemed to me that I was working on Caitlin Boss in ways that Jack, sunk into a crowded couch downstairs within my view, would approve of. It was all about persuasion.

As for the seeming cold-hearted nature of my coup, please don't assume that we public radio folks boast a higher agenda than our commercial radio colleagues. That's retro in the extreme. We may have started out way back in the paleo-radio days with the sound of *MISSION* ringing round our heads, but we're grown up boys and girls now. We and our commercial friends often swap jobs, and the only significant difference left between us, I am pleased to say, is...well, I cannot think of a significant difference. With a beer-foamy hug of my waist, Caitlin Boss agreed to back me when I sprang my coup at Tuesday morning's management meeting.

Our general manager tries to give the impression of being hang-loose (he claims that even the buttons on his cuffs are too constricting for him), and he sometimes gives lip to spongy words of consensus and compromise, but I know him for what he really is, a powermeister whose ambitions are loftier than his ideals. If he is ever to rise to network

v.p. he first needs his radio station to succeed. And
nothing, to coin a phrase, succeeds like success. I
knew he would find a way to implement the
profitable, if seismic, changes that his program and
marketing directors were hammering for, even in the
face of howling, hemorrhaging protests from the other
managers. After hearing all sides, he thought it over
for two weeks, then privately directed me to plan on
expanding NPR talk to eleven, and to offer Jack
Silverstern the following: 1. the evening board shift,
including local cutaways; 2. a Jazz show from eleven
till one.

"You mean I come on every half hour and do
the weather and that jivey shit?" Jack said when I
dropped the news on him. He was sitting across the
desk from me with the door closed. He looked like he
was about to short circuit from anxiety, and – how's
this for pathetic irony? – he was wearing one of his
famous aloha shirts, inspired by the Oscar-winning
performance in *From Here to Eternity* by guess who.

"Maybe every half hour," I said, "maybe less.
I know it's not much, but I wanted to find a way to
keep you on staff. And you would still be doing *some*
Jazz." For once, our conversation was not a banter. I
did most the talking.

Jack was too shocked to respond. After all
these years? So suddenly and arbitrarily cut loose,
like a beloved and productive veteran pitcher
inexplicably put on waivers. He said he had to think
about it.

"You've got time," I said. "The changes don't
go into effect for another six weeks."

"After the fund raiser."

"I need to know sooner if you're with us. The offer's good so long as you say nothing about the changes on the air. I can't let it become a public fact."

Jack looked at me in disgust. How could I expect anything from him but the coolest ON-AIR stoicism?

"I know you won't," I said.

I thought I knew what Jack's response would be to my offer. The humiliation would be too great. He would have to say fuck this jivey shit, make a tape and put out the word. I was partly right. He didn't quit, but he cut an audition and let it be known to a couple of p.d.s that he might be available.

Jack's fame had long ago spread among radio execs up and down the coast, so a good offer came forth almost immediately. It was for weekday Jazz host, nine to three, at a university O&O. The pay was probably ball park with what he got from us. It was a decent gig, if you set aside that he'd be working around students, and that 9:00 A.M. would call for some macro biorhythmic adjustments. The only real drawback was that it was in a town six automobile hours away.

Would he accept the job and leave? A vigil of sorts began. It was hard to read Jack. At times he was enveloped in a dark funk of betrayal, and I was sure he would quit if only to return the insult. But at other times he was drawn ever closer in bawdy camaraderie to his fellows, including me, as if he wanted me to see that he understood the merciless side of business as well as the next man. At these times, I thought he might choose to swallow his reduced status with us and tough it out.

But the larger question, maybe the only question, was between Jack and Delphine, and there was no telling what was going on between them. Jack wasn't around the station during the day anymore. I never saw them together. But look, seeing as we have a primary source here on the other end of the modem, why don't we pose the question to her. Delphine, darling, tell us please what was happening with you two during those "deciding" weeks?

*

You're asking me? Not telling me? You actually think I'm going to tell you the private things that went on between us? Like, did we consider trying to carry on a long-distance romance, or whether I should move with him and try to get a job once we got there, or just break it off altogether? Is that what you're looking for? All right, Mr. P.D., if you want the truth, what happened was – sex happened, and in a big, big way. I know this will give you a good hoot, that Jack and I hadn't gone to bed before. There had been good reasons why not and not all of them had to do with my illness. But then, you pulled your awful stunt, and with me starting to recover we just both decided separately that now was the time. Maybe all that betrayal he felt set off his sexual appetite. You know, when everything else is out of control, here was something he could do well in a lot of different ways. Frequency. Duration. Control. Oh, I'm intellectualizing. Let's just say we fucked like animals. But it was also more than that. For me, some way or another, it reunited me and my body and Jack all at

*once. It was transcendental. Does that answer your
question? I'll leave it for you to imagine all the things
we did, and I'll bet you'll imagine them just fine. I'll
say only this much, it was nothing like what happened
with us in our mistake. Take that home and sleep on
it.*

*

My error for asking an impertinent question.
But never mind. This matter of should he stay, or
should he go was decided one evening while Jack was
on his way to work. I learned about it mostly from
newspaper accounts, but I've pieced together bits
from Delphine, and, knowing Jack, I can fill in some
other likely details.

Dressed in fedora and scarf, Jack stopped at
Nick's for his usual dinner sub and twenty minutes of
over-the-counter sports banter with the proprietor.
Then, climbing the sidewalk steps he was confronted
by a teenager in a cube cut and a black sweat shirt cut
off at the shoulders. It was obvious to Jack what the
kid wanted the instant their eyes locked. The kid had
a pistol pressed against his black pant leg at the knee,
so it might not be seen from a distance. It looked like
it could be a slick metal toy, but Jack had seen
enough guns to know it was for real, a .38, a piece.
The priming pin was cocked. Jack must have seen it
coming; must have stood there with his bowels
clenched, knowing he was about to get *greased* out
here on the sidewalk in view of who knows how
many people. There would be nothing to it. It would

be just another terrible thing that happened, except it would happen to him.

"I don't have anything," said Jack. "I just spent my last money on this sandwich. You can have it, but I don't have any money." Was this Jack's Chicago street smarts showing through? The fact was, Jack had $32 in his wallet. He may not have known the exact amount or been aware the wad had shrunk quite so small, but Jack always carried cash. Did Jack sense that the sight of money might inflame this kid to do something insane? Was he that cool in such a tight circumstance? Or was he just stupidly defiant?

The kid looked at the outstretched paper bag. His eyes were black and empty. As it turns out, the kid was entirely capable of doing the worst. In the newspaper the next day the police said that the unidentified juvenile they held in custody had twenty minutes before robbed a man at an ATM three blocks away and shot him three times in the stomach. The man was dead. Each time he pleaded for his life, the kid had shot him again.

The kid snatched the paper bag from Jack's hand and ran like hell down the street.

Jack eventually did come to work that evening, after giving his story to the police. I didn't see him, but I listened in my office part of the night. Jack, as always, maintained an impeccable cool. In fact, as good luck had it, I saved, shall we say, Jack's last skimmer tape. Here's a cut: "That's Duke Pearson's... 'Jeanne.' Cannonball Adderley recording made in, ah, 1960 in Chi-ca-go. Cannonball Adderley on alto sax, his brother Nat cornet, Barry Harris piano, Sam Jones bass, Lewis Hayes on drums.

Voyeurs   DJB

Seventeen past nine, Jack Silverstern with you, you know we do Jazz here every weeknight from seven right up to one o'clock in the A.M. For music next, we have, lesee, Benny Carter, 'sat O.K.?"

Next afternoon, Jack called to say he had decided to take the gig at the university O&O and was taking a few comp days immediately. He said he knew this would leave me somewhat in the lurch to get a replacement on such short notice, but I sensed he also didn't give one fast fart. I was relieved. The conversation was curt. He left me with the impression that I would see him again, which I have not. That night I scheduled Jack's time-generic back-up program. We were tape all night. I wonder if he listened to himself.

I'm sure Jack and Delphine took a good stab at love on the telephone, but it wasn't long before Jack got himself settled into his new station as the cool jock who'd come from a successful, big city 30,000 watter. And it wasn't long before Jack, working around pretty co-eds all day, his nights free, sort of let things between him and Delphine unravel without much effort.

The programming changes are working almost better than expected. There was of course some initial listener outrage brought on by our cutting Jazz completely, but this was weathered well enough, by simply ignoring it.

Delphine seems determined to make something of this job of hers, which in fact she is doing, as I have been assigning her more interesting work lately. She has regained most of the alert, taciturn energy and disarming appearance that tipped me off balance in the first place. A slight floral scent, yes. She may be angry now, but I can be in alignment with that. It's nothing fatal.

ON DRINKING

I am teaching myself to drink. This is strictly Emersonian self-reliance. I don't want any help. I seek no truck with toffy-nosed connoisseurs who instruct on which liquors taste best and which are best suited. This is my Dummy's Taste Test, where taste matters only a little. For this dummy, it's the high that counts.

Kind reader, you may ask, why at my late age, now that the illusions of my thirties have faded like steam on a bathroom mirror, am I teaching myself to drink? For that matter, why forchristsake haven't I been drinking all along? Perhaps we'll find answers along the way.

For now, the event of the moment. Here follow my initial findings of: *The Bartel Dummy's Taste Test of Distilled Beverages. (TBDTTDB)*

I have restricted my research to the whiskey shelves, amber mashes only. That's a real man's drink. Thus, the kissy, foul-mouthed barflies who nightly sit beneath the TV, so they can be alternative entertainment, sharing martinis and suckface, will find no help here. Like they need any help from me. I have also avoided sweet liquors – Frangelico, Drambuie, Sambuca – and all lip-smacking exotics. These are for party drinkers, not everyday pounders such as my sneering, lynx-eyed friend Sean who slams shoulders at my favorite hammered-tin bar.

Moreover, wine, being its own sub-culture, is omitted from TBDTTDB, as is beer, with its soda pop buzz. A true drinker like Sean, the kind to which I submissively aspire, can put down five ambers, neat, in an hour and give nary a thought to pissing. Try doing that with five draft pulls of Sam Adams, which brings us to our first rule of the manly art of drinking: *Never leave the bar for the bathroom.*

Jameson (Irish Whiskey) The cream of mash. Jameson passes my lips like a whispered confession, at once acrid and delicious. But more than taste, Jameson delivers me to a high of creamy nostalgia. I view the past through a sepia tint. Late one night last winter, as rain chanted its gray litany out on the sidewalk, I sat drinking Jameson alongside Sean. The wings of his nose were touched with pink. At some point deep in our conversation, the good toad said to me, "Sadness – it's the sane reaction to this life?" I identified the quality of this observation as substantially informed by both Larkin and Jameson, for the creamy mash likewise offers me its cradling arm and helps me down the crooked road to the past. Jameson enfolds sadness in a blanket of barley. It buffets. There's a reason the Irish are weepy-hearted ole sods. 'Tis the drink, laddy.

Tullamore Dew (Irish Whiskey)
To my buds, T-Dew brings more of an urban bite to the first kisses off the lip, spiked with anxiety and fear. But that's just my *objective opinion*. Subjectively, Tullamore brings back to me bedside lamp-lit images of my tawny haired Irish lass, now long beyond my grasp, Anne Elizabeth. AE rarely spoke above a whisper. Dogs were instinctively drawn to her. She

used to call me after hours from work to complain about her chump-husband, and during our long phone talks she curled up on the floor in the well of her desk, or so she told me, and I believed everything Anne Elizabeth told me, as the counselor believes the counseled. AE and I did not drink together, though when together we were intoxicated. When AE and I got together it wasn't for drinking, so this is not a case of simple association: the flavor of T-Dew and the taste of AE's unadorned lips. Rather, Tullamore's complex mash delivers a hushed, exquisite high which somehow summons her Irish ivory skin, and her mouth in a small astonished oval.

Seagram's 7 (Whiskey) Calls itself "a blend of distinctive character." Part of the blend of this dark amber American mash (which comes in an even darker amber bottle as if hiding something) must be metal shavings. Has this stuff been aged in Haitian oil drums? Is that what's distinctive? Seven Crown rattles off my palate. The aftertaste is like sucking a rusty bedspring. Likewise, its high is blunt and slams my eyes with a stunned look. At least it's cheap. Recommended for head bangers and hockey fans. My cousin Vickie used to drink 7. She is a big bad strong woman. Her first husband was a skinny guy, and inside two years Vickie threw him through the front door screen onto their porch and out of her life.

Jack Daniel's (Kentucky Sour Mash Whiskey) Corn-fed goodness. I was introduced to Old No.7 by Joe (his real name) the bartender at my favorite nicked-wooden bar. Joe has a salt and pepper beard that tapers to his navel, like a Sikh's. (I know such beards. During my twenties I lived among turbaned Sikhs, who did not cut their hair or drink whiskey.) Joe wears no turban. He's bald, soft-spoken, politic, gentlemanly. Rides a monster bike, a cell phone in his shirt pocket. One late night after hours, I sit at the bar drinking JD's sour mash with Joe's wife, TJ, who owns the joint. She tells me, incredulously, that Joe answers his cell phone even when on the Interstate. "He'll shout, 'I can't talk now, sweetie, I have my helmet on.'" Joe looks over at us from down the bar and gives a grinning thumbs up. Sour mash is matured in oak casks with charred insides, but Jack's "sour" designation is deceptive. The more I drink, the sweeter it kisses the tongue. It invites more. The high is kick ass, daring, which for mild old me means shouting at the NFL as it plays out its dramas on TV. Joe, who has no personal history with sports outside ponies, sips a diluted Jack behind the bar and works up the occasional lather for the home team, if he can determine who that is, as a courtesy to his (his wife's) customers. It's sweet of him.

"What's the difference between Scotch and whiskey?" asks my friend and former student Paula one night at my favorite carved-wood java bar. Well, I say, the answer is an interesting compound of things, and the moment between us is not right for a discourse on malt and Scotch grain whiskeys, and the mash of pre-cooked maize. She has stolen this time to see me; no time to speak of what happens when malted barley gets blended with unmalted cereals.

"I bet a lot of cereals wanted to blend with barley's malt," says Paula, who typically speaks with similar crackling intelligence & wordplay.

Then there are single malt whiskeys, translucently represented by **The Glenlivet**. I suggest this was the likely drink of the simplifying Ralph Waldo, or, if not Emerson, then his drinking buddy Henry David.

There's also rye and corn Canadian whiskey, such as **Windsor Canadian**, which is distilled under strict supervision of the Canadian Government to produce a lewd, leering high.

"You've been on one of those the last half-hour," says Paula, wife and comely mother of three.

I could go on, but no, instead I remember the second rule of the manly art of drinking: *All things come to one who listens, not to one who pontificates.* (That goes for free drinks, too.) With Zen-like sparseness, I say to Paula, "Scotch is a blend. Whiskey is straight." Paula gives me a look as if she has

something important to figure out
and takes a sip of the Dewar's I
bought her, squinting hard.

Dewar's (Scotch) It's true, Scotch
snaps the tongue more acutely
than whiskey. But after a few sips
of this pale amber, Dewar's flows
like a Robert Burns lyric. *The
landlayd and Tam grew
gracious/Wi' favors secret, sweet
and precious.* Dewar's delivers me
to an alert, pensive high. It offers
interesting ambiguity. A pleasing
blend of action and inaction. The
past is far; I am more in the here
and now. On this night, sitting at
the carved-wood bar of this java
joint, Paula brazenly rests her hand
high on my thigh and kisses me
below the ear. I look ahead to the
makeshift stage, where a husband-
wife duo with guitars plays tunes
by The Byrds. Paula takes my
earlobe between her lips, yet I
display the manner of a manly
drinker, stoic, not indifferent, but
not responsive, revealing nothing
to people up and down the bar who
perhaps do not have someone of
their own to suckle their earlobe.
That's where Dewar's comes in. It
increases your empathy even as it

emboldens your self-will. I may be sitting on the bar stool with my spine straight as a USMC Sgt's, but I am also alive to her precious touch. Smiling Paula, graced with a fine Dewar's high, knows this and kisses me again. She cares not who sees.

Johnnie Walker, Black Label (Scotch) Coats my teeth like extra virgin olive oil. Black's illicit aftertaste expands in the nasal cavities. Think of Sade's hips. No extra virgin drinks Johnnie Walker, neither Black nor younger brother Red. The high is empowering. One spring night at home, at my computer after a single John Dub-ya, I e-mailed my cyber lover, who may or may not be a young woman of Wyoming: "As Richard Burton said on his death bed, 'I regret nothing.' So it is with me."

Johnnie Walker Black is the drink of my attorney friend Joyce. As she sits at my favorite chrome, swank and bluish-light bar, wearing a silk shantung suit, a glass of gold-patina rocks at her ready, Joyce projects The Total Package: *I manage an in-house staff of over fifty. I can handle myself on a sailboat, and I have good taste. Who are you?* As we sip Black together, Joyce tells me she has a list of twenty-five things she wants to do in life. "I keep checking them off as I do them. I checked off hiking the Northville-Placid Trail last year. Self-sufficient for two weeks in the Adirondacks." Joyce has no alcohol with meals. A pre-meal JW Black satisfies all her drinking needs.

J&B (Scotch) Enjoying this ultra-pale amber is a hard-won reward. The taste at first does not invite, may even repel. It slowly sidles up to the tongue. Before long, it can become "the only drink." The high? Remember Ricki Lee Jones with beret and brown cig? *Now it's J&B and me/That sounds close, but it ain't the same./But that's okay/Hot City don't hurt that much.*

Being a mash scientist, I recognize in those lyrics J&B's unique gut-check high. As it happens, TBDTTDB began with several bottles of J&B, drunk with my former wife J, as we sat across our floral table-clothed kitchen table, during the grim final stages of our long, childless marriage.

J&B seemed to be the only thing that would get her to talk about her slow withdrawal from me, and J&B may have been the only thing that helped me swallow it, until the day she left. I haven't so much as sipped it since.

Jim Beam (Bourbon) Often confused for the above, Jim Beam is a darker amber, a more honeyed mash, and delivers a friendlier (some say less clear-eyed) high. I have chosen to introduce this sweet Southern bourbon to my new honeyed friend Erin, at my favorite hammered-tin bar. Erin may be young, but she is no novice imbiber. She both works the bar and patronizes the bar. Yet, whiskey of any kind has not been her drink. Jell-O shots and beer are more like it.

When reaching over the bar to serve drinks (I bow in reverence as I say it) the adorable young woman possesses God's own most astonishing artistic achievement, or, if you are a non-believer, the most perfect and magnificent ass in my paltry life. Greater than Mozart. Better than Bauhaus perfection. More awesome than the

Grand Canyon. That's not just the Jim Beam talking. I would give up drinking for one fistful of that booty.

But everyone, man and woman alike, admires Erin's curvaceous slopes behind the bar. I also watch Erin alight about the bar as a paying customer in slimming summer dresses, in search of animated conversation. Over weeks, we have a few mouth-to-ear exchanges in the noisy joint, but mostly pink-eyed Sean is hitting on Erin and monopolizing her crawl about the bar. Finally, though it was a hard blow to his ever waxing & waning ego, he realizes he's just too damn old (52 to her 25) and now assumes the role of mentor. He tries to warn her about me. But it's too late. Erin and I have formed a *manage-a-trois* here in the bar. She and me and Jim Beam.

Erin drapes her slender arm over my shoulder as I sit at the bar and tells me close, "I want to be someone who knows." Her Beam-breath is heavy near my ear. "You know. I want to know what you know."

"Very well, daughter, I will tell you the words of the Old Sage, as they were told to me. Ready your pretty shoulders 'cause here it comes. The Old Sage says, 'Life goes on.'"

She lets this sink in like the barroom profundity it is, and then with a naughty turn of her head says, "You want to know what I know?"

"Yes. It is why I came here."

And so Erin walks me up the street to my townhouse and teaches me.

I now think I should instead caution Erin on the vile truth about drinking Jim Beam, or any of the other ambers I've delivered into my system these many months, in the manner in which I have drunk them. For you see, in search of the high, over the taste, I've been compelled to keep drinking each liquor until I reach its high. I am proud to say, fellow seekers, that I obtained those peaks many times, and when on high I recorded what I found, mapped it out, distinguishing one high from the next. Alas, it is also true that my scientific efforts were slowed as each amber landed me on the couch the next afternoon for two hours of hateful drowsing before the big screen TV (the last present I gave J).

Which is why I am sore afraid to administer my TBDTTDB to **Wild Turkey (Bourbon)** 101 proof. By comparison, its potent country cousin Jack Daniel is 86. The Gobbler perches on the highest, far back shelf, shunted out of the way for disuse, yet ironically assuming a place of honor, on high. A drinker must make a long climb to reach the Turkey.

My genius poet alcoholic friend Mark (now dead for years) made the legendary climb. In the short years at the end of his life, when he was sober, at the mention of Wild Turkey Mark smacked his lips. "Smooooth, the finest," he remembered. Thanks to Mark, Wild Turkey and Shakespeare are inseparable for me. Every chance he got, or created, Mark quoted the Bard at will, not as an actor, but as one saturated with the Moor's rage, stoked with King Henry's testosterone, haunted by the same shadows as the Danish prince. "No more," went Mark's Hamlet, "and by a sleep to say we end the heartache and the thousand

natural shocks that flesh is heir to."
Mark's utter Bardness was one of
the phenomenological wonders of
my empirical existence. I
remember the days and nights
when Mark most brimmed with the
Swan of Avon. It was when he
consumed 101 in wondrous
quantities. I swear upon
Shakespeare's Collected Works
that I, as a young man who did not
drink, once sat across a fold-up
metal table in Mark's stink kitchen
and watched him break open and
consume a fifth of Turkey in one
hour, and then was astonished to
hear he could still speaketh the
English tongue, articulating tropes
of Mercutio. "True, I talk of dreams,
which are the children of an idle
brain, begot of nothing but vain
fantasy."

That, Mr. & Ms., is a drinker.
To him, I bend the knee, and
perhaps a test on the Gobbler may
be in order after all, soon, for the
sake of research.

And for research's sake,
here follow, in brief, additional
TBDTTDB findings.

**Crown Royal (Canadian
Whiskey)** The Yukon's idea of

Fine De Luxe. Gaudy, broad-shouldered bottle, husky taste. An honest, expansive high.

Maker's Mark (Bourbon) A slow-sippin' Kentucky mash, excellent with mint. The high focuses my meticulous concentration. I marked up many a *Racing Form* with Maker's as my betting buddy. About broke even.

Southern Comfort (Is it Scotch? Bourbon? Syrup? What?) Defies boundaries. Sweetened with molasses and Mississippi mud. An erratic high all its own. Sometimes you know what you got 'cause it makes you feel good, other times it's a ball & chain.

Disclaimer: All of the above research compiled by TBDTTDB is subject to individual life circumstances.

So, you want to hear the circumstances that led me to teach myself to drink in the first place? Nah, you don't want to hear about that, do you? Besides, I think I heard Last Call, so let us forget all that and put our lips to a glass of **Old Grand Dad (Bourbon)**, on the rocks. A gum-singeing medicinal first taste, which grows whisker-soft but never quite cozies the tongue. The high pulls me inward. I can sit at any of my favorite bars the thirty minutes required to put away two Old Grand Dads and no one will speak to me, thank you please. My world is reduced to the pool of yellow-amber before my nose.

Which brings us to the third rule of the manly art of drinking: *Here is your watering place. Drink and be whole again beyond confusion.* Hey, kind reader, tell me, I forget, was it Frost, or Old Grand Dad told us that?

Voyeurs   DJB

ASHRAM ETHICS

To TKK

The first crisis to arise at the ashram involved a nest that appeared in the eaves of the front porch. Several birds, identified by Ishwara Kaur as sparrows, were gathered up there and creating a white-speckled mess on the porch and steps. "I guess they missed their exit for San Juan Capistrano and wandered up the coast aways until they heard the song of the Guru being sung during sadhana."

As days passed the mess spread as more birds gathered in the eaves. Around the table at evening lungar, some members of the sungat made complaints, especially Siri Sat Sangeet Kaur and Mukia Sadarni Sat Simran Kaur. Not only was it unsanitary, they said, but it gave a poor first impression to those who visited the new ashram, which had so far included several mukias from Preuss Road. It was also a bad first impression to be giving to the neighbors, many of whom had lived half-a-lifetime in Long Beach and appeared wary of the ashram. "It's a bad impression just to people just passing by," said Siri Sat Sangeet Kaur. Indeed, the mess had grown so that it was as clearly visible from the street as the name GURU TEGH BAHADUR ASHRAM painted in savadar-blue script above the porch.

Voyeurs   DJB

Sat Darshan Singh, whose karma yoga included the upkeep of the front yard, recognized that even if the complaints may not have been directed right at him, he was the person in the best position to receive them. He climbed a ladder to investigate.

The nest held four eggs. "Three are baby blue and one is brownish with yellow speckles," Sat Darshan reported to the sungat, his large forehead scrunched with paternal concern.

Instead of removing the nest Sat Darshan promised to the rest of the sungat that he would hose down the porch every evening when he got home from work. He followed through on his promise for a week, smiling satisfyingly the whole time. But it did little good. Even before the water on the porch was dry, white splatterings began to reappear.

Meanwhile, Siri Sat Sangeet Kaur continued to complain, and late one night her complaints escalated. She was in the Shakti quarters after *Kirtan soliha* removing her turban when she discovered bird droppings. She bounded downstairs red-faced and indignant, and burst bare-headed into the kitchen, interrupting a mini-sungat confab of five, demanding that the nest come down first thing in the morning after sadhana.

"Sat Nam," Sat Darshan responded. "Ji, that's someone's home up there."

Siri Sat Sangeet Kaur plowed through his words, "Well can't we at least just move it someplace else then?"

Gurupukh Kaur said she liked hearing the cooing coming from the front porch.

"Fine," Siri Sat Sangeet Kaur said, turning to face Gurupukh Kaur directly, "then let's just move it someplace where Gurupukh Kaur can still hear it. In the tree outside Shakti quarters would be fine with me." Gurupukh Kaur looked on solemnly, unblinking. Siri Sat Sangeet Kaur continued again to speak to Sat Darshan, "Put it anywhere. Just not on the porch."

Ishwara spoke up to say she happened to know that when a nest is disturbed the mother bird rolls the eggs out onto the ground and abandons the nest. "Maybe we could wait until the fledglings are old enough to fend for themselves?" she said.

"I agree with my wife," said James, leaning on his shoulder against the large refrigerator like he remembered doing at parties in grad school.

Seeing that she would find no support here in the kitchen from her fellow sungat members (Siri Siri Kaur sat on a stool over by the juicer and had said nothing), Siri Sat Sangeet Kaur turned abruptly to go, issuing a cursory "Sat Nam, jis" as she left.

Over the next few days, she would not be dissuaded from her complaints or her demand that the nest come down, but whatever support within the sungat she had at first was dwindling. Even Mukia Sadarni Sat Simran Kaur, despite her personal distaste for the mess, now sided with those who would leave the nest in peace.

Siri Sat Sangeet Kaur stopped her complaints. Instead, she began entering the ashram only through the back door, and each time she came frumping into the service porch she loudly called attention to the inconvenience she was being forced to suffer, stomping her feet as she removed her shoes, huffing and puffing.

This had little impact on the sungat's tolerance of the nest and tended only to irritate people. Ishwara took to chanting *Wahe Guru* each time Siri Sat Sangeet Kaur started in. It helped to soothe the irritated soul, hers and her friend's.

But not everyone was so gentle with Siri Sat Sangeet Kaur. One afternoon, Siri Sunderta Singh, in the kitchen where he'd scooped up a bowlful of wheatberries, shouted at her as she snorted disgust in the service porch, "Shut up, ji! Let the poor birds have their life!"

Siri Sat Sangeet Kaur complained to Mukia Sadarni Sat Simran Kaur about this rude outburst and the mukia intervened, meeting with them together in the sadhana room for a sixty-minute Satanama meditation, to calm matters.

It so happened that Siri Sat Sangeet Kaur soon received unexpected support from Siri Siri Kaur – unexpected because Siri Siri Kaur usually had nothing to say about anything. She was a pale, shallow-eyed, scrawny woman of about twenty, with a two-year-old daughter. She appeared somehow auraless. A year ago, she had entered 3HO over the wretched protests of her Palos Verdes parents, who, according to Siri Siri Kaur, believed their daughter had joined a cult. At first, she was living in Guru Ram Das Ashram in Pasadena. That's where the deprogrammers caught up with her, or nearly did. Siri Siri Kaur claimed her parents had hired men to snatch her and her child out of the ashram. She was sure of it. She had proof. Twice the two men parked up the street from Guru Ram Das and sat in their car for hours. They were twice seen hanging around the Gurdwara Sahib on Preuss Road, but only on the two times that Siri Siri Kaur had come into L.A. for Sunday Gurdwara. Once they followed her on foot to the 3HO co-op and might have snatched her right then and there had she not become frightened and asked for a savadar escort back to the ashram. Another member of the Guru Ram Das sungat, a man who was in law school at UCLA, checked into their identity and discovered they were notorious among the Divine Light Mission community. Siri Siri Kaur threatened her parents that if they didn't call off their deprogrammers she would take their granddaughter and disappear into an ashram somewhere else in the country, or the world, where they wouldn't find her. The deprogrammers stopped coming around.

Siri Siri Kaur's daughter was likewise named Siri Siri Kaur. Yogi Bhajan named the child after the mother. At first, to avoid confusion some members of the sungat began calling one Big Siri Siri and the other Little Siri Siri, but Mukia Sadarni Sat Simran Kaur nixed the practice. She said that Yogiji hadn't named them Big and Little, and no doubt for good reasons. "Who knows what kind of vibrations are created in your aura by having `Big' or `Little' in your name?" said the mukia.

Besides, as James thought, how could you call Siri Siri Kaur "Big" when she was so slight and quiet she scarcely parted the air?

Siri Sat Sangeet Kaur offered her solution enthusiastically, "Why don't one of you go by your full name *Siri Siri Kaur Khalsa*, and the other just by *Siri Siri Kaur*. Call Little Siri Siri Kaur by her full name. That way she can get used to hearing herself being called Khalsa."

This seemed like a viable solution, until Siri Siri Kaur herself, revealing a surprising strength of defiance, announced that *Siri Siri Kaur Khalsa* was too long a name for a mother to be whispering in a child's ear, and besides Siri Siri Kaur was confused enough as it was, now that she'd lost her non-Sikh name, Misty.

Mukia Sadarni Sat Simran Kaur's solution to this small dilemma, which she said she had discussed directly with Yogi Bhajan, was to call the mother *Siri Siri Kaur* and the child *Siri Siri.*

One morning after sadhana, Siri Siri Kaur was out on the front porch, rocking in the swing and dreamily enjoying the early sunshine. Siri Siri was left to wander around on the dewy lawn. After spacing out awhile Siri Siri Kaur looked over to see Siri Siri eating moist bird droppings off the steps. Before she could climb out of the swing, get down there, and pick up Siri Siri, the child was pelted by a dropping on the back of the neck and broke into a loud baby wail.

The next day, at the weekly sungat meeting after Sunday Gurdwara, Siri Siri Kaur, holding a bunch of flowers in her folded hands, asked if the sungat would reconsider whether the nest on the porch was really such a healthy situation after all. The whole sungat was present – twelve, plus the child – and Siri Siri Kaur was visibly uncomfortable speaking up like this before everyone. Sitting next to her, Ishwara, who held Siri Siri, leaned slightly toward her, offering body-language support. Siri Siri Kaur said, "I'm no longer sure myself. I think I now agree with Siri Sat Sangeet Kaur that something should be done. Siri Siri could have gotten sick if someone wasn't there to stop her."

Siri Sat Sangeet Kaur, who was sitting by the big couch with her legs tucked beneath her like a chubby former debutante, quickly climbed to her knees and took the floor. "I don't see why some people in the sungat have to be just so caught up in their egos that they'll allow the health of the sungat to come after their need to act all life-affirming just about a bunch of birds. Sikhs take care of their own first. Certainly ahead of animals. At least that's what Yogiji would say if he were part of this discussion."

Now Siri Sunderta Singh, sitting in half-lotus next to James, added his support: "I mean, we're not Jains are we? It's totally ego to say we're above all violence. The Khalsa tradition began in the first place by having to be violent. It was a matter of survival. It's part of our heritage. Even Yogiji says violence is a fact that exists in the human being. Sometimes it has to be."

"Nobody's talking about violence," said a grim-mouthed Gurupukh Kaur, in what she must have meant as a neutral tone.

"Sat Nam, ji, but we *are*," insisted Siri Sunderta Singh. "You have to get right to the root of the issue, and the root of the issue here is violence."

James thought that from what he had been able to tell during these first weeks in the ashram Siri Sunderta Singh was not one to hold to a conviction for very long. Perhaps not coincidentally, in the five years before joining 3HO Siri Sunderta Singh had been, under various names, a converted Catholic, an engram-measuring Scientologist, a Sakta worshipping various female forms of the deity, and a devotee of Satya Sai Baba and the sadhu's magical gray ash *vibhuti.*

Whatever the merits of the arguments of Siri Sunderta Singh and Siri Sat Sangeet Kaur, they were put forth with holier-than-thou vehemence enough to sway some of the sungat. A vote was taken. Six of twelve voted to remove the nest, including Siri Sat Sangeet Kaur, Siri Sunderta Singh, Mukia Sadarni Sat Simran Kaur, Siri Siri Kaur (who said she thought Siri Siri should have a vote, too, and would want to vote to get rid of the nest, though this was not allowed), and Kirpan Singh and his wife Pungit Kaur, both of whom had once been health workers of some kind and so, they said, could identify with Siri Siri Kaur's concerns for her child. The other six voted to keep the nest.

Mukia Sadarni Sat Simran Kaur, in her best parliamentarian mukia voice, began issuing the decree that insofar as so many members of the sungat wanted the nest taken down, and insofar as the mess had progressed to the point that it presented a potential health problem, and insofar as it reflected badly on the sungat in the eyes of others – including some Sikhs in certain circles on Preuss Road who already had the idea that "the beach sungat" might turn out to be a little laid back when it came to household karma yoga.

"But it's a tie," James interrupted, breaking his usual sungat meeting reticence. "Don't you think that unless we have at least a simple majority who want to take it down, we should continue to try to find another solution?" He didn't like his own pseudo-parliamentarian tone, a faint echo of the mukia's.

Suddenly it was settled when Ishwara spoke up to say that she was willing to change her vote.

James looked at his wife, confused.

"Sat Nam, Ishwara Kaur Khalsa!" said Siri Sat Sangeet Kaur.

Mukia Sardarni Sat Simran Kaur gave the chant, "Wahe Guru ji akal Khalsa."

The sungat, with Siri Sat Sangreet Kaur the loudest voice, gave the response, "Wahe Guru ji ky fatah."

Later in their bedroom, James asked Ishwara why. She said she was sorry she had to do it, but she knew Siri Sat Sangeet Kaur well enough to know she wasn't going to stop agitating until she got her way. "But really," said Ishwara, "I just feel that more than anything else right now it's important to keep harmony in the ashram. And Siri Sat Sangeet Kaur was right about one thing. A lot of the reason we wanted to keep the nest was because our own egos were getting in the way. You could see people building up righteous anger over it. But anger is just anger whether you think it's righteous or unrighteous. It's still tied up with your ego, of having something and not wanting to give it up."

"Her bit about *other people's egos* was the part I thought she was most wrong about," said James.

"I know, ji. But maya comes in many different forms. We just have to know to recognize it."

Late Sunday afternoon, Sat Darshan performed the sad chore of removing the nest from the eaves. Taking it in his large, thick hands, he lifted it gently from the eaves and peered in. "Five eggs," he informed the trio gathered around the ladder (Ishwara, Gurupukh Kaur, James). Sat Darshan carried the nest to the back yard. James hauled the ladder back there and set it up against the tree outside the Shakti quarters. Sat Darshan climbed to the highest limb he could reach and placed the nest in the crook. As best as anyone saw in the next several days, no birds came near it.

BOUDOIR

The sunlight, a bright late-winter white, reflected off the stone steps. Heat-flecked. It felt good on her face. She closed her eyes as they brimmed. Warmth spread across her cheeks and cradled the tips of her ears. Lingering with Diane outside Shaffer Hall, Beth meant to squeeze every minute from her lunch break. The sun was saturating her three layers and warming her shoulders. She undid the top two buttons of her blouse and bared her throat. This, thought Beth, feels even better than my full-spectrum lamp.

She wondered why she could never be around Diane more than a few minutes before feeling the need to confide something. It was just a way that Diane had. She was easy to talk to. Beth wasn't ashamed to admit she was old-fashioned when it came to personal matters; closed-lipped. But when she got around Diane she felt different. She confided in Diane a lot. Not that it was exactly mutual.

Diane never revealed much about herself. As far as Beth knew, Diane's home life with her investment counselor husband and their two Corkran Middle School honor students (boy and girl) was something right out of Nick-At-Nite.

Diane stood next to her passively, holding her wrist, looking out at the brownish lawn of the quad and the gangly spines of trees against the white sky. She was ten years older than Beth and her supervisor at Continuing Studies. At times Diane had acknowledged the imbalance of confidences between them. "I live just such a dull life next to yours," she would say after Beth divulged one of her little secrets.

Beth had another secret that she'd been aching to tell Diane for the past hour, since they sat down in the Basement Cafe over twin tuna salad croissants and Cokes. All through lunch it was all she could do to stop herself from blabbing about it. Now with the warm sun pouring over her she decided, why stop myself? Diane is my friend.

"You'll never guess what Nat told me he wanted for his birthday," Beth said, pulling her compact from her handbag, popping it open.

Diane paused before answering, her glasses glinting with sunlight." I'm sure I couldn't," she said.

Beth powdered her high-boned face with a swift circular motion, an excuse not to look at Diane as she talked. "He wants me to pose for one of those boudoir pictures. You know those. You see ads in the back of magazines. There's nothing to it really. It's not like it's illicit or anything." She checked the small flip in her bangs, dropped the compact into the handbag and closed it with a resolute click. She turned to face Diane, assessing her reaction.

Beth had been with Nat for eleven months. Living with him, that is. Before his separation there had also been a few months. Lately they'd been going through a sexual heyday of sorts. Their love making had actually grown more intense, which was saying something considering the charged sex on the sly they'd started with. Now it was, well, Beth felt awkward discussing it, but "acute and incredible" was one way she put it. All this Diane knew from past confidences.

"Your amorous hijinks," said Diane, laughing to hide her embarrassment. "Sounds like good clean fun to me." She felt herself blush guiltily the way she did whenever she witnessed others making fools of themselves.

"He told me this morning – after I broke the ice," said Beth. "The whole weekend he gives me the silent treatment because of some argument we had Friday night. Not a word the whole weekend. He mopes around the house with his TV sports and his music. I mean, I don't put the whole blame on him. I admit I was in on it too. But this time I guess I needed to show I could give as good as get. But this morning I decided enough is enough. His birthday is coming up and I didn't want things to be tense for that. So I broke the ice."

Diane was not about to ask what happened between them Friday night. She detested gossip. If Beth felt she had to talk about it, fine, she was there to listen. But she wasn't asking. She had a good idea anyway. It most likely involved Nat's daughter Melanie. The little girl (she was eleven) lived with her mother. Nat had her every other weekend. Beth sometimes complained that Nat was

"mortally attached to that girl," whatever
that meant.

"You know what he says to me?" said
Beth, turning back to the warm sun. "He acts
all hurt and he says, 'You're talking to me?'
It's his Robert De Niro. He says, 'Three days
of nothing and all of a sudden you're talking
again, to me?' I could have brained him."

It happened in their wet-bar sun room,
the "sunken room" as they called it because it
was down three steps. The early sunlight was
leaking through the venetian blinds. Nat sat at
the round wooden table with, as Beth saw it,
his instruments of ablution: a bowl of crunchy
cereal, a coffee cup and the newspaper folded
in quarters.

Nat had a slender frame, like he was
strung together with wire. His hairline was
receding, undeniably, but otherwise, as he
liked to boast, middle age had not got to him
yet, not "thickened" him. He could be a man-
boy in that way, just as when he wanted
sympathy he adopted a slumped shoulder
sheep dog look. It usually worked on Beth,
especially in the morning before he'd tied his
ponytail and his gray-mottled hair was spread
across his shoulders. That's how she found

him when she came downstairs, and she knew then that it was all right to talk. Despite the wretched weekend she wasn't really ready to brain him. She was so relieved to have their awful silence broken, and he looked so adorable, that what she really wanted was to eat him up that instant. She had to break the ice, she told him, slipping onto his knee, because, silly thing, she had to find out what he wanted for his birthday. She expected him to come out of his shell slowly, to shrug and say he didn't know what he wanted, or he didn't have time for that nonsense. Instead, Beth's eyes widened in surprise as he straightened his shoulders fastidiously and told her without hesitation what he wanted for his birthday. He even knew of a photo shop that worked with a local publisher. It specialized in boudoir photography. "The guy's shown his work in a few galleries," said Nat, "mostly in the west. And he's been in a few artsy erotic magazines."

"You sound like you've checked this out pretty carefully already," said Beth.

"Not really. I just happened to know about this one."

Beth squirmed inside with this new and sudden idea of Nat's. She was always a willing and interested participant in anything he wanted to try in bed, which involved some pretty interesting circumstances that she hadn't confided to Diane. But it was one thing to lose herself in bed with him. This was another thing altogether. "I don't know," she said. "I'm not sure I could. I mean, in front of another man?"

She could see that the mention of another man acted like an electric current traveling through is body language. In an instant he stifled it. He rubbed his palm up and down her back and laughed his fifteen-years-your-senior laugh. "Baby, sweet baby excuse me my low p.c. quotient this morning, but as a statement of fact you are simply not going to find many *women* doing boudoir photos."

Beth smiled and slipped off his knee. She picked up his empty bowl. Nat gave her a quick pat on the bottom. She knew it would not be long now before his whispered obscenities began, of how he was looking forward to giving her a good fucking, or spanking, or whatever he had a yen for. Beth slipped from his grasp and stepped to the sink at the bar. As she rinsed the bowl she beheld herself in the small mirror bracketed to the wall. How is it, she thought, that things always smooth themselves out between us without a word spoken? It's not like they avoided things. It's more like everything has been wordlessly forgiven on both sides and what's the point of discussing it? Beth thought this was one of the wonderful things that she had with Nat. Sooner or later they always got back on the same wave length; got cemented back together. As if nothing had happened. It was their chemistry.

And what *had* happened Friday night? Beth never considered it any big deal really. Word had got back to Nat, via Joyce naturally, that during Melanie's weekend visit Beth slapped her face. It was true. She had slapped her. Fat on the kisser. The sullen, foul-mouth brat needed to be slapped and Beth considered it only fortunate that an adult happened to be on hand to slap her. Not only had she been sassing back, as always, but this time she actually spit on Beth. Where did kids get off with that kind of behavior? thought Beth. She would have never been allowed to get away with something like that when she was a kid. So what Beth wanted to know was just how was a responsible adult expected to react under such circumstances?

She twirled her long hair round her fingers and tossed it over her shoulder and turned at the sink and gave Nat the coy look he liked so much.

"I'll think about the picture," she said, "seeing as we're on speaking terms again. Maybe I'll surprise you." But then, wishing to leave him with a spoonful of doubt, she frowned and added, "Just don't go counting on it too much."

She started up the steps out of the sunken room, his voice clipping at her heels like a small dog. "You're the one asked what I wanted for my birthday..." Beth didn't need to turn around to see Nat's predictable expression, the slumped shoulders, the sheepish pout, what a sweet thing, "...well *that's* what I want."

*

With each passing day the prospect of a boudoir photo dimmed for Beth. She wanted to make the photo, for Nat's sake, but she couldn't bring herself to call the photographer that he picked out. It seemed like such an ordeal now. But time was running out and one day she saw an ad in the *City Paper* for a photography studio. It was surrounded by ads for Jewish Matchmaker, Hot Talking Personals, and one for a brochure on how to contact adults who like to wear diapers and baby clothes. "Ick," Beth said aloud at her desk.

BE DAZZLED PHOTOGRAPHY promised "a relaxed atmosphere ... professional make-up/styling ... be a covergirl or centerfold!" There was an unsmiling woman reclining on her elbow, wearing a black negligee that revealed an immodest amount of bosom. "For goodness sakes," said Beth, staring at the ad as she listened to the phone ring on the line. She knew the approximate address. It was one of those old office buildings downtown. She pictured herself in an upper-floor office-cum-studio, wearing the lavender baby doll and filigreed panties that Nat bought for her, posing in the harsh glare of a bank of lights, straining to look seductive to some man, a stranger, behind a camera. It was ridiculous and humiliating. Then a man answered, and Beth knew she couldn't go through with it. She hung up.

On Friday, two unrelated things happened. Nat called to say that this weekend he was flying to Orlando to take Melanie to Disney World. He was even taking the first half of Monday off from the store. "It's about time she saw Disney World," he said, "and Christ if I'm going to let anyone else show it to her for the first time." Nat believed that Disney World created an unhealthy fantasy for children; distorted their emerging understanding of reality. He wanted to protect Melanie from it, which meant confronting it head-on. Then he added, his voice turning cautiously ironic, "And we wouldn't want to run the risk of you two repeating your last little performance, would we?"

Beth felt perfectly relieved not to have to face the little brat so soon. "I'll miss you," she said.

The other thing happened twenty minutes later. Diane stuck her head into Beth's cubicle to ask if she'd mind handling a preliminary interview with a photographer who wanted to pitch a course for the fall term. As Diane's assistant, Beth handled these sorts of chores all the time. They were easy. You just listened and asked a few standard questions.

"I'm just so swamped with things that absolutely must be finished or I can't go home tonight," said Diane. Of course, she was not so swamped. She was too organized for that. But she'd guess that Beth probably had not followed through on her boudoir photography idea (or she would have said so) and that maybe an interview with this photographer whose resume was checkered with unusual freelance credits might turn into something. Diane felt not a little guilty, and not a little sneaky. But she liked Beth and wanted to help, at least in this small way. Anything more would be too much like butting into Beth's private affairs.

The photographer, Dawn, was a heavyset woman of about thirty-eight. She had puffy hands. Her hair was severely cropped, and her unhealthy olive skin appeared stretched tightly across her unflatteringly plump face. And if Dawn looked bad to Beth when they first met in the outer office, once they sat down in Beth's cubicle, awash with anti-depressant light, Dawn looked, well, ugly. Beth had to watch herself from showing astonishment. Thick fatigue pouches hung beneath Dawn's gelatinous eyes. Rolls of fat bunched at her middle, visible even beneath an oversized, buttoned khaki jacket, freshly ironed. She talked in a flat, self-deprecatory whine and wouldn't look Beth in the eye. Now and then she tried to smile, but apparently smiling was not Dawn's thing at all.

Yet for some reason that she could not put her finger on, Beth soon found Dawn comfortable to be around. She listened attentively as Dawn made her pitch.

She stumbled often over words. She was vague on details. Who was the course aimed at? "Anyone interested in photography." What level of expertise was required? "None, or a lot, doesn't matter, everyone's treated differently." What kind of photography? "All kinds. I do it all, or whatever they pay me to do, ha ha." What exactly would be taught? "How to take pictures."

Beth knew the interview was not going well, but she still liked Dawn. As Dawn began to talk about her specialty – working with "available light" – Beth had the uncomfortable thought: Is it so impossible that I like this woman partly because her appalling looks make me feel prettier? Certainly, Beth considered herself pretty. She was petite with button features. She sensed that when she got old, very old, her face might look gaunt and angular, as if her bones had turned to glass. But for now, she was pretty, and she knew Nat appreciated her beauty. Nat was a great one for appreciating her. "My pretty one," he called her.

But oops – her thoughts had drifted from the interview. Dawn seemed not to notice that she wasn't being heard. Suddenly Beth felt a lump of empathy rise in her throat. Suddenly she needed absolutely to get *something* from this interview that would allow her to recommend this ugly woman to Diane for a second interview. She asked Dawn why she wanted to teach.

"I've been trying to make it go for five years," Dawn said, her teeth on edge. "But with this economy and everything, freelancing just doesn't pay the bills." Then with moist self-pity filling her eyes she added, "I guess

you know how that old song and dance goes?
You probably get it all the time."

No, Beth did not get it all the time, and
she did not know how it went. Most of the
Continuing Studies courses were taught by
confident young professors looking to add to
their vitas, or older professors interested in
teaching something out of the ordinary.
Freelancers were rare. Personally, Beth would
never dream of freelancing at anything. The
very idea was distasteful. Others in the
office, such as Diane, felt freelancing had a
romantic aura. Charting your own path, or
whatever. Beth's definition of a job was one
that came with regular hours, benefits and
vacations. Call her old-fashioned, for all she
cared. She had enough uncertainty in her life
without having to worry about where her
paycheck was going to come from. "I
sympathize," she said to Dawn. "It takes a lot
of courage to pursue something like what
you're doing because you believe in it."

"I wouldn't go that far," said Dawn. She
nervously fingered the lapel of her khaki
jacket. "It's what I do. It's what I want to do.
And I hate working for other people. That's
about it."

Instinctively, Beth demurely touched the lapel of her own jacket – a black linen number from Saks, worn over a pink Oxford shirt. She realized what she liked about Dawn. She saw a hint of the same defiant My-Way mentality that she so admired in Nat. Back in the terrible days when Joyce was putting up an unspeakably vile fight over the separation, it was this quality of Nat's – a certainty that he knew what was best – that Beth clung to see her through. Nat seemed to will things to happen, and they did happen. He knew how to get what he wanted, and to Beth that was the sexiest, most dazzling thing she had ever seen, just like the way he was imposing his will on her to get her to make this boudoir photo, asking for it in that sheep dog way, then saying no more about it, but expecting it, in the way he looked at her, in the way he took for granted that she would do as he wished, no threats, no pleading, just assuming, *expecting*. Each time Beth saw this strength in Nat she wanted more than anything to do whatever she could to help make it happen for her man.

"Do you do portraits?" Beth asked Dawn.

By the time they parted in the outer office, shaking hands like business partners, they'd agreed to meet tomorrow at two, at the house, for what Dawn called "the shoot." Beth said she'd have the place to herself, and, if they were lucky the sunlight at that time of day through the bedroom window could be just right.

*

Joyce was a big-boned woman with prominent breasts, a hefty woman. She had handsome features – a long jaw and striking, dark, sad eyes, though they hadn't always been sad. Her full face, she thought, might go either way as she aged; become more handsome and distinguished as with certain men, or, as she feared, go flaccid and begin folding over on itself, as with many people who drank. Nat was her opposite. As a couple they looked as if she did the eating for both of them and he watched, uninterested.

In the past few years Nat had twice forced Joyce to go to AA. The first time it almost stuck. Eight months, dry as a whistle. But Nat himself would never stop drinking. He wasn't the one with the problem. If anything, sitting on the rear stoop after work nursing a bottle of Boh was one of his few sources of nourishment.

Temptation got to Joyce. She came out on the stoop, took a seat beside him, inching him over with her hips, opened a cold one for herself, and things, as they always found a way of doing, sort of unraveled.

After that Nat kept up a sniping campaign for her to go back on the program. Joyce responded by getting drunker, stiffening her resistance to him. As a precaution, Nat opened an account at another bank and began siphoning into it. Christmas Eve was the clincher. They sat at the kitchen table all night wrapping presents, with two bottles of Old No.7 between them, arguing sotto voce about the same tired subject. A CD of Mozart piano concertos was playing continuously in the living room, mostly to muffle their voices from their little girl upstairs.

By morning, as their little girl could be heard stirring in Christmas anticipation, they each had a strained throat from angry whispering and Nat was threatening to take

Melanie and go. Joyce cursed him, loudly, her voice cracking. She knocked an empty glass to the floor, a sudden shatter. "Threaten all you want," she said, suddenly standing, glaring across the table at him with sodden eyes. She didn't believe one god damn word he said. She dared him.

So, he did. Late one morning two weeks later he pulled Melanie out of her third-grade class and drove off with her for New Orleans. Left a note. After two days Joyce heard from him. It was 1 a.m. He was calling from a motel outside Bogalusa. He said he wasn't calling to have a discussion. He was calling to *tell* her something. Joyce listened mutely, eyes stricken. He could picture her; knew which phone she was on from its crackle. She was standing in the kitchen, holding the olive-green receiver the way she did, between thumb and middle finger, her other thumb stuck in her mouth. Nat told her that the next time he called it would be for one reason and one reason only, to get the name and phone number of her new sponsor. "When you're back working the program that's when *we'll* be back."

Joyce was cool; not sober but coherent enough. "Can *I* talk now?" When he didn't say anything, she went on. "First of all, you'll be back when your vacation time runs out, the vacation time that we could have taken as a family, that maybe could have made a difference in all this. I know you, you inhuman bastard. What are you doing with my kid? I want to talk to my daughter!" He hung up. She threw the receiver at the wall where it left an olive-green scuff. She cursed him. The next morning, she knew the routine, she checked herself into detox.

It was true, Joyce did know him. She knew about Beth from the first, or, lacking evidence, felt it. Each time Nat and Beth met – usually at her tiny apartment a few blocks from her parents' house, but sometimes, as Nat's special treat, in a room at the Sheraton downtown, across the street from the book store cafe that he managed, and where after making love (oh, but it was more than making love, Beth had done that before enough times, this was entirely different, it was sweet carnal ecstasy, just fuck and fuck and fuck, she could not get enough of this wonderful man who fit so perfectly inside her, dear

Lord) after making love they fed each other
the hotel's courtesy chocolates which had
been tossed to the floor with the bedspread –
Joyce would greet him at home with drunken,
aggrieved accusations and things thrown. Of
course, he denied it, called her crazy, and it's
true she didn't know who or where, but she
knew her husband's every nuance. She knew.

When at last she found out who, from a
so-called girl friend who had known for weeks,
she went to Beth's parents and confronted
them in their living room. The two of them sat
together on the sofa, looking stunned and
embarrassed, with the same lemony eyes, like
aged siblings, wearing pastel nylon exercise
suits from their evening walk. On this evening
at least, Joyce was sober, by force of will.
She *would* remain in control of herself. She
said that of course she understood how her
husband might be attracted to a pretty young
woman like their Beth. It was only natural for
a man at his stage in life. But this was a family
here. There was a little girl involved. She'd
brought along a picture – Melanie in her yellow
dress, her sharp hazel eyes alit with the
childish joy of having her picture taken. Of
course, Joyce didn't expect Beth to walk away

just because – she started to lose it – just because *the wife* objected, but surely they saw what a mess they all had here, and surely they saw their own responsibility in helping to put a stop to it.

For the first time Joyce noticed that the floral print of the sofa matched the tasseled drapes. How she hated these people.

Beth's father, a sloped shouldered man with pattern baldness, shook his head slowly, his lips pursed in distaste. "It's wrong what Beth's done," he said slowly. He said they would talk with her. But what really were they to do? She was an adult. They couldn't force her.

When Nat heard about Joyce's "little performance" he announced he was moving out, to an old brick apartment complex near Hopkins. It was not a divorce, he told Joyce, only temporary. To Beth he said that instead of them having to run off to her place she could now walk over to his place anytime.

Two weeks later Joyce abandoned their house and moved with Melanie into the same complex, two floors below. She began showing up at his door at all hours, banging violently so that he had to let her in, if only to keep someone from calling the police.

One night, on the shadowy landing outside Nat's door, Joyce confronted Beth coming up the stairs. She blocked the way with her broad, strong body, her dark eyes boring into Beth's skull, moving closer, smelling of whiskey. "You and your store-bought tan," said Joyce.

Beth stood her ground three steps below, hands stuffed deep in the pockets of her baggy sweater, eyes wide, seeing more than they could instantly comprehend.

"What I want to know is," said Joyce, "what is it that you, you filthy cunt, why are you so intent on destroying my family?"

Beth fled. She called Nat from a pay phone on campus and told him she couldn't come there anymore.

Nat threatened Joyce with divorce. "A real divorce! None of this separation crap!"

Now it was Joyce's turn to use Melanie as a pawn. After weeks of drinking she got sober again, by her own unaided efforts. Once she'd been sober for six days she threatened to take Melanie and go live in another state.

"You won't see her again until she's an adult, I promise you."

Nat and Beth spent a long weekend afternoon talking in her tiny apartment, cuddling on the sofa. Nat explained that he didn't need and wasn't seeking complete custody of his daughter, but Christ if he was going to lose her either. He had a solution, but Beth, his pretty one, would have to trust him.

Beth kissed him, a smooch on the cheek, then softly pressing against his mouth, the way he most liked. "Of course I trust you." But when she learned of his solution, she didn't know what to think.

His solution was to take Joyce to Myrtle Beach for a week, just the two of them.

Melanie was handed over to Joyce's mother in Silver Spring. Nat and Joyce checked into an oceanfront bungalow, and the first thing he pulled out of his suitcase was a bottle of Old No.7. Joyce took it was a peace offering. Each day at dusk the high tide crashed against the boulders ten feet below their balcony.

After four days, Nat called Beth at work. He only had a few seconds to talk, he said, but he wanted to reassure her that everything was all right.

"Is that so?" said Beth, steadying her voice. She cupped her hand around the mouthpiece. "You're there with her, and you're telling me everything's all right. I see. And are you" – the muscles in her throat stiffening – *with* her?" She heard Nat choke down a laugh with his head turned away. "Nat? What? Are you drunk?"

"Yes I am, my pretty one, but I'm not the only one. So let's leave it for now by saying things appear to be headed in the right direction. It's hard for me to say, you know, sweetie. Listen. I've got some friends moving my things into a place I've rented. It's in South Baltimore. It's all set up. I want you to think about moving in with me."

Beth thought it was an awful trick, but it worked. Nat, upon arriving back from Myrtle Beach, moved into a two-story townhouse on the other side of town, in an ultra-urban neighborhood where rehab had only just begun. That first night Beth came to visit. She was unnerved by the look of the area – the huddled brick buildings, the crumbling sidewalks. She found Nat exhausted, his face molten from sobbing. But he was grateful, he said, that she'd come to him.

Joyce harassed him on the phone at the store, but after a few days she stopped. Nat surmised to Beth, "She's starting to feel unbearably humiliated about the messages she's leaving." It took her almost three weeks to track him down at the townhouse. By then Nat's attorney had initiated legal action. Nat anticipated that Joyce's lack of sobriety would work very much against her in the eyes of the court.

And it did. The judge ordered a joint-custody arrangement until details of the divorce were finalized. The girl would live with the mother, but the father was granted equal say as to all important decisions. Regarding visitation, the parents were to set a schedule for themselves, but the father was awarded a minimum two days a week. Nat opted for less than the minimum: a weekend every two weeks.

*

Like she hoped, the sunlight was perfect. Sharp and clear. She couldn't have been more pleased when, as she finished up the bedroom, putting her scruffy Ally Bear in the bureau drawer ("In you go, you bear"), smoothing the peach down comforter, lugging the black exercise bike into the bathroom and draping her lavender baby doll over the handle bars. Dawn was due in ten minutes. White bands of finely edged sunlight shot through the bedroom windows.

She ran through her mental list of things to do and remembered one she hadn't checked off. She needed to get some chips and Coke at the store for Dawn. She herself hadn't had anything to drink since early that morning, on purpose. There was a baby doll in her future. But it was important to Beth to be a good hostess. She threw on her baggy sweater over a t-shirt and automatically checked for the mace in the pocket. Nat once made her swear to God never to walk in this neighborhood, day or night, "without the mace *in your hand*."

Out on the sidewalk, walking in the shade of the weathered brick houses, she felt the air slip its cold hands inside her sweater.

She gripped the sleeves in her palm and walked with her head down. She didn't have far to go.

She had tried to give no hint of her plans to Nat. "I'll be home all day," she told him. "Call when you get to Orlando." She felt illicit, which she thought wouldn't hurt when it came time to do it.

On the corner outside Sam's Grocery were three boys, the kind Nat derisively called whitebread rappers, dressed in cowled sweatshirts, bright-colored sweatpants and sloppy sneakers. One of them was palming a cigarette next to his thigh, sneaking a smoke out here in plain view of anyone who cared, like anyone did. The other two boys were sharing a cigarette, the one taking a puff, the other standing expectantly. They passed it back and forth like a joint.

Beth suddenly felt self-conscious in her floral leotards. If Nat were here, she thought, he'd give these kids a big "What's happenin', bros?" and a sarcastic wink. And she could give Nat's ponytail a stroke of solidarity.

The two boys sharing a cigarette took lewd notice of her. She looked away quickly and ducked inside the store.

She liked coming here. It was closer than the 7-Eleven and had an old-time air about it, a smell of dank wood, a low, dark ceiling. A Korean family ran it. Every square foot of available space was filled. The aisles (all two of them) were so narrow you had to keep your elbows tucked in as you moved. Beth dropped into an easy crouch in front of the upright dairy case. Balancing herself with a hand on the door, she selected a large bottle of Caffeine Free *diet* Coke. As she rose and turned around to the counter, which was no more than a small opening carved out of the merchandise, a little girl burst through the door and hurried and wedged herself in front of Beth. Rude little girl, thought Beth. She was about eight and should have been taught some manners by now.

The back of her hair had been tied in cornrows, by fingers that seemed to lack both skill and patience. On tiptoes the little girl could barely see over the counter. She dropped a crumpled pack of Kool's on the counter without a word. Her other fist was packed with coins, which she spilled on the wooden surface. Her mother, thought Beth, is probably home in front of the TV.

The woman behind the counter, who was about Beth's age, was wearing a plastic wrap on her hair. Beth was amused. The woman wordlessly counted the change, tapping each coin quick with her fingertip, and scooped it up. She put a Kool's on the counter and the little girl snatched it and dashed out the door was fast as she came in.

Lying open on the ledge of the register was a small Bible. At least Beth guessed it to be a Bible, the black cover, the thin pages, gilt edges. The script was Oriental. Beth's eyes remained fixed on it as she bought the Coke and chips. She waved off the woman when she reached for a plastic bag. Beth never spoke to the people who ran the store. She had never heard them speak English to other customers. She assumed they didn't.

Once Beth was back out on the gum-stained sidewalk one of the boys, the one with his own cigarette, cooed in her direction, "Yabba dabba doo." The other two chortled. These little boys are harmless, Beth told herself. When she felt she was a safe distance she gave her bottom a little shake. This got a round of teenage yelps and grunts.

It's time, she thought, to start getting in the mood.

Across the street was parked a shabby, dark green van. The sunlight highlighted its nicks and dents. The old bumper sticker on back read TAKE PHOTOS, NOT DRUGS. This has to be Dawn, Beth thought, tugging her sweater closed against the cold.

The engine started. She wasn't leaving? Beth hurried across the street, glancing for traffic. She held her elbows close as she ran, tightly hugging the Coke and chips in either arm. She felt so shaky running. Her body was not one for athletic coordination. She had never run worth a darn – though in her dreams she sometimes ran, on and on. Just as often she leapt into the air and flew. It seemed no less fantastic.

She reached the van and saw that, in fact, it was Dawn. She rapped her knuckles on the window.

Dawn looked over, betraying a pinch of theatrics, her face gray through the glass. She rolled down the window. "You're here. I thought maybe you'd got cold feet or something." She sounded both relieved and irritated, whining either way with the same brown breath of melancholy. "I thought maybe you'd decided to avoid me."

Beth tried to laugh it off. "Of course not."

"Yeah, well, I thought you were."

Dawn climbed out of the van and walked around back. She was wearing the same oversized khaki jacket, buttoned, though it now looked like it had spent the night wadded in a ball. She said she had some equipment she could use help with carrying into the house. She opened both doors to the van. Inside was crowded with lights and stands and cases and rolled up screens.

"I didn't realize you were going to use a lot of equipment," said Beth. She certainly didn't like the thought of making a big show for the neighbors.

"It's not a lot," Dawn huffed. "Here, grab one of those."

Beth set the Coke and the chips on the curb and dragged a heavy stand out of the van.

It took three trips to get it all into the house, parading across the street. Next, they hauled it up the curved staircase. "So much stuff," Beth said, puffing, once they got it into the bedroom. There was hardly room to stand. "Weren't you going to use – you said you used available light, didn't you?"

"I do," said Dawn, unhappy with the question. Her face was in shadow, just above a band of sunlight. A gray face. "But sometimes you need extra light for certain effects. Back lighting, things like that. Besides, the sun'll be gone soon." Changing the subject, Dawn said that coming up the stairs she noticed the pictures on the wall of Beth and Nat together. "I didn't know you were with *Nat*. You should have told me."

Beth was worn out. She slouched on the bed and sank into the comforter. "You know him?" It was no real surprise. Nat maintained a large coterie of book store junkies.

Dawn bent at the waist and reached around her middle to set up a tripod. "Sure. I'm in Connolly's all the time. How long you been married?"

Beth put her head in her lap and thought a moment before answering.

"Oops, sorry," said Dawn, "I didn't mean to automatically assume –"

"No that's all right," Beth said into her lap. "We've been married a little while."

"Where is he? Is he here? No, I guess not, or he'd of helped us with the stuff. Will he be around? I'd like to say hello."

"He's out of town."

"Oh," said Dawn. "Too bad."

Beth softly kicked her legs against the bed, the floral pattern of her leotards against the peach. She remembered that that morning Nat was in a hurry to leave. Beth wanted to snuggle. She was feeling very fuckable. And she thought having their funky smell in the bed would probably help later. But Nat was quickly up and showered and dressed and headed out the door, even though, as she knew, and she knew he knew she knew, his plane wasn't for another five hours. "You know how it'll be," he said, kissing her quick on the lips. "She won't be ready. Joyce will've done nothing whatsoever to help and I'll wind up having to get her packed." And he was gone.

Straightening out of her slouch, Beth put her hands in the pockets of her baggy sweater and felt coins. She realized she had left the Coke and the chips on the curb. It was probably gone by now. She looked up at Dawn. "Are you going to be long setting up?"

she asked, trying to bring lightness to her voice.

"No," said Dawn, irritated. "Why?"

"Nothing. No reason. Look, maybe I'll go get changed."

"Good idea."

Beth went into the bathroom, which was crowded from the exercise bike. Her lavender baby doll hung limp from the handle bars. She climbed onto the bike and sat slumped. She's here and it's already started, she thought. Just go through it, you big dope. Do it right. Think sexy thoughts.

She sat thinking for several minutes, listening to Dawn set up. Finally, she undressed and slipped into her silk baby doll, beholding herself in the mirror. The baby doll looked more revealing than ever. How can I wear this, she thought, in front of anyone but Nat? But wasn't that the whole point? It *would* be Nat. Nat's eyes would be all over this photo. Her hair was tousled from all the lifting and climbing. Good, she thought. It makes me look like I just got out of bed. Nat likes that look a lot. Still, she tied a floral bow in back and tidied up a little with a hairbrush. She added a touch of powder to her upper cheeks with a swift circular motion and dabbed some of Nat's Joop! on her the hollow of her throat. Just keep thinking of him, she thought. She watched in the mirror as her hand moved slowly down her belly. It slipped inside her filigreed panties. Only for a moment, she thought. Just enough to conjure up Nat. A moment later a hard tweak of her nipples helped bring them to life. For good measure she touched them up with lipstick. She pulled her saffron robe over her shoulders, cracked open the door and peeked.

Dawn was holding a light meter close to the bed. Beth couldn't help but notice the sprawl of Dawn's butt. The men's Levi's didn't help matters. Dawn turned and motioned with an irritated wave for Beth to come. "Let's get started here. We're missing the best light."

The orbit lamp on the bedside table had been turned on. Beth sat on the edge of the bed within the soft globe of light. As she had feared from the first, disrobing in front of a stranger was going to be hard. She told Dawn to hold on one more sec and hurried out of the room.

"Hurry up," Dawn called after her.

Down in the kitchen she opened a magnum of Bordeaux and filled two goblets. She leaned back against the sink and vigorously massaged her clitoris with three fingers, really working it, till she began to lather. She came back to the bedroom holding the goblets like trophies.

Dawn looked at them disdainfully. "Not while I'm working."

Well, all right, that was fine with Beth. She'd have both. She took a gulp and walked around the bed to the clock radio on Nat's side and dialed up some public radio jazz. Another large gulp of wine. She climbed up on the bed, curling her legs beneath her, and slipped the robe off her shoulders. She told herself to stay focused on Nat, pretend it was *his* eyes upon her, *his* appreciative and lustful eyes. Be his pretty one.

"Is that how you want to pose?" said Dawn. "Or what do you have in mind? Are there parts of you you want to accentuate or something?"

"I don't know," said Beth, shifting position, the comforter crinkling. "I guess I thought I'd leave that to you. But let's see. Nat does tend to like my backside a lot."

Dawn took some Polaroids. Beth struck a few different poses, trying to move sensuously to the music. Now the photographer in action, Dawn kept up a running chatter. "So I guess you decided to keep your own name. That's funny, you don't seem like the type."

"Huh?" Beth had been concentrating on the honey sunlight and the feel of Nat's hands upon her. "Why not? I mean, what type?"

"Oh nothing," said Dawn. "It's just a feeling. Nothing personal. I have a habit of forming opinions of people real fast. It's something you have to do when you're a photographer. You got to figure out what kind of person someone is, really fast, so your pictures will bring out something of who they really are. I'm usually right though."

"I see," said Beth.

"So why did you?"

"Did I what?"

"Keep your name?"

"I don't know. Someone else had his already, I guess."

"Oh. Divorced. I know what that's about."

This conversation was definitely deflating Beth's sexy thoughts. "You've been divorced?" she asked.

"No, but I know how it is."

Dawn laid out the Polaroids on the bureau and together they looked them over as the clarity emerged. Beth sipped wine. Dawn picked out two poses, one lying on her side, sort of Kinski-esque, and the other, funkier, propped on her elbows and knees, looking over her shoulder. "The ass shot." said Dawn.

Beth downed another gulp of the rich red liquid and agreed, "Yes, those are good."

The sunlight was almost gone. Dawn said she had to a few lights. Suddenly instead of honey sunlight the bedroom was flooded with light – bright and hot. At first it was a rude blast in Beth's face, but soon the heat began to feel good on her skin. She began perspiring pleasantly beneath the baby doll. And better still, she could no longer see Dawn from the glare. With the help of the wine's warm glow she managed to tune out Dawn's chattering and return to her sexy thoughts, imagining Nat standing beside the bed, his erection in his hand, speaking nasty things to her, telling her what he had a yen to do to her.

Suddenly Dawn laughed, a freakish burst of sound like a bark. "I just remembered I was in Connolly's a few days ago and caught Nat in rare form. You should have seen him. He was really giving it to this assistant prof." Dawn said the professor's name, Roorda. Beth had heard of him, someone in the history department, but he didn't teach in Continuing Studies, so she hadn't actually met him.

From a semi-crouch behind the tripod, Dawn snapped four pictures clickclickclickclick. "You should have seen it. This poor chump was going on and on about all the things he was doing in order to keep some woman from getting tenure. That's right, her name was Eve Somebody. He was going to all these lengths to get other faculty to vote against her." Clickclickclick. "Nat listened to this for a while, then he says, 'So are you up for the same tenure slot?' When the guy said he wasn't, that he was doing all these nasty things just because this Eve was a terrible teacher, Nat scoffs and says, 'Oh, I see, a man of principles.' You should have seen the chump shrivel up right in front of everyone."

Dawn laughed again, an ugly barking laugh without mirth. Clickclickclick.

Beth had heard Nat tell lots of jokes about academics. He said he got a perverse pleasure out of "bringing the educated assholes down a notch." It was one pleasure Beth didn't share with him. She reached the goblet from beneath the orbit lamp. The wine wasn't helping anymore. She was growing depressed. She tried to fight it, to be sexy no matter what. She bit her knuckles the way she did when Nat made her come. But it was no use. She felt ridiculous. There was no denying it: she was smack in the middle of the very scene she'd sought to avoid – in her baby doll sprawled before a bank of harsh, glaring lights, making eyes at some stranger behind a camera, as humiliation rose in her throat and congealed to a lump. She thought of the boys on the corner chortling at her, and how she teased them. Her eyes burned. She bit her lip to stop from crying. Oh, this was awful. She didn't feel sexy. She felt stupid and demeaned. And there was also no denying that it was Nat who'd put her here, manipulated her into this, as surely as he manipulated everything else.

"Very nice," said Dawn. "You look like you mean business. Why don't you try turning over now and let's get a few of that ass shot."

And she did. She rolled onto her elbows, cocked her head over her shoulder, pulled her hair away from her face and positioned her shapely buttocks in the air, because, well, because she knew that this was the picture Nat wanted. She tugged at her panties, revealing an extra inch.

It was dark outside by the time they finished. Dawn promised she would drop off the contact sheets at the Continuing Ed office on Monday. (Nat's birthday was Wednesday.) Dawn asked if when she came by did Beth think she could maybe introduce her to Diane?

Beth shrugged like it was nothing. "Of course." She took the second goblet with her into the bathroom and decided to stay there until Dawn hauled all the equipment back down to the van. She sat on the exercise bike in the dark, her right hand tucked under her left armpit. She sipped wine. She wanted to cry. But she didn't quite cry, not then, not until later that night, when she was alone, sitting in the sunken room with all the lights on, after she'd finished most of the magnum, after the phone rang and, as she'd half expected, it was Joyce, calling from Orlando.

"I didn't want you to miss out on what it feels like," Joyce said with more than a pinch of vengeance. "It's only right you should know when he's doing it to you."

*

Monday delivered a raw blue morning. As promised, Dawn arrived early at Shaffer Hall with the contact sheets. But Beth wasn't there. She'd called in sick, so she could face Nat when he got home. Dawn, sensing an opportunity, insisted to the receptionist that her package was important and if she couldn't give it to Beth personally she wanted at least to give it directly to Diane.

The receptionist phoned Diane, who came from her office. She accepted the envelope from Dawn, who said it contained some items which Beth was waiting for. The two women chatted briefly. Diane told Dawn she was pleased that someone like her, a freelancer, was interested in teaching a course for them. She said she hadn't had a chance yet to speak with Beth about their interview, but she certainly would when Beth returned. At this, Dawn became dour and tongue-tied.

Diane took the envelope into her office and laid it on the desk. It was clasped but not sealed. She had an idea what it might be, and she wasn't about to open it. But then she asked herself what if it really was something important? Maybe she'd better open it to make sure it wasn't something to which she herself could attend.

She blushed guiltily but did not return the contact sheets to the envelope until she examined them all. She told herself: remember to act surprised when Beth confided in her about them.

SOLDIERS
IN THE HOLY LAND

Dear Mira,
       You know how travel can loosen your tongue. When you're far away under a foreign sky you talk about things which at home you'd choke down the moment they came up. But while traveling – that's different, especially when your travels bring you into the arms of one so attentive as you, my sweet. If I must put it in writing instead of telling you face to face, well, maybe that says how hard it is for me to talk about. I need to be alone to talk about it with you.

It has to do with what you were saying this afternoon as we sat together in the shade on our rocky Galilee hillside. You say the Holy Land seems overrun with IDF soldiers. "Thick as locusts," and I agree. They're in cities, towns and settlements. They're on buses and beaches. They're along roadsides hitching rides and in markets muscling their way to the front of the line.

You said it best, dear one, even with sub-automatic rifles on their shoulders many of them look like children. To me, many others look like insolent teenagers who've been forbidden by their parents to talk back. That is what they are after all, teenagers, drafted right after high school, men and women, everyone but the most devout. The men get three years compulsory, the women get two.

They sling their weapons around amongst the citizenry like they've never heard the words "accidental homicide." But you're right, just as many of them look like children, many of them *are* children. I've seen a young woman licking a soft ice-cream, with lavishly fussed-over hair in tight ringlets, and a pink and gray stuffed elephant pinned to the pants pocket of her olive drab uniform. I've seen a young man who has yet to start shaving wearing paratrooper wings over his breast pocket and a Bart Simpson key chain attached to his belt. Their faces, despite the military makeover, are those of innocents. Mira, in your tender way, you are appalled by them, "toting their guns."

Of course, among the horde there are also many true soldiers – hardass grunts standing straight and silent as cypress trees. They are older, twenty, twenty-one, and not to be messed with. They've had their maturity hastened and become what the others – the children, the insolent teenagers – will become to one measure or another, for the Israeli Defense Force demands it.

If it must be said, I'll say it: Israel, surrounded on three sides by enemies and on the fourth by the sea, would not be here today were it not for her soldiers. And yet, I agree with you. Something seems to have been taken from these young men and women. They will emerge from their years of service inevitably changed in ways that they may or may not have chosen, if given a choice.

Which brings me, finally after much shuffling, to what your kind touch and gentle prodding has caused me to want to tell you. It has to do with the ordeal that long ago slammed the lid on my own youth and that has since left me contorted as one of our gnarled olive trees.

To speak plainly (for really at heart I am plain), I'm talking about going to prison after refusing to be drafted. I don't mean to sound highfalutin or self-righteous. I'll admit, I've washed myself of guilt in the private waters of self-righteousness a time or two, or two-thousand, but I wouldn't want to subject you, dear one, to *that* embarrassing display. The facts are simple. It happened in 1970, and at the time I didn't feel very righteous about it.

At the end of high school, I won the lottery. My birthday was drawn third. I wonder if back then you were still too young to have paid much attention to somber matters like America's handpicking of her infantry. Did you feel the silent ripple of fear that ran through the hearts of Majority families like mine? Well, I paid attention, I felt it, because for someone like me number three in the lottery meant only one thing: I was going to Vietnam.

It was nothing less than expected of me. My father, a man of few words and strong opinions, had been a Marine in The War and fought the Japanese on three islands in the East China Sea, Okinawa included. My brother and only sibling Andy had already served a tour in Nam – a name he uses readily to this day but blanches when I use it. So you might say, and Dad did say it, our family had a history of doing its duty in defense of our country.

Still, the first thing I did was begin looking into the usual legal options of evasion and compromise. I found out fast that they were not much open to me. We were working class, and even if we'd had a mind to, there was no way we could have mustered the influence to keep me beyond the long arm of the SSS. A college deferment was moot. Except for my straight A's in baseball I had not been a good student and wasn't headed for no Stanford or Berkeley, or even to any of the L.A. commuter schools like Cerritos Jr. or L.A. State. Besides, as I understood, these diploma factories were little more than amusements along the freeway where the education you got was no more enriching than what could be had at other off-ramp amusements, say, Disneyland off the Santa Ana or Winchell's Donuts off the San Diego or Golf N' Stuff off the 605. Not that I, who had struggled for my 1.4 GPA, was in a position to condescend to any form of higher education. I had also known two boys, older than I, who enrolled in school hoping to win a precious deferment but nonetheless were yanked into the Army quicker than they could say Ho Chi Minh.

Finally, I considered the National Guard, but at the time that domestic branch of the United States Armed Forces was being deployed on campuses across the land, and only two months earlier had marched onto one in Ohio and fired into a crowd of protesters. Four Dead. I would have none of that.

By swift elimination my options were made clear. Either I left the country with familial scorn upon my head and without hope that my government would ever allow me to return, or I went to prison – besides the unspeakable option I would not choose.

So now, my adorable, sympathetic sunshine, I want to try to say why I chose as I did. Was I filled with moral outrage at Nixon's War, at Kent State, at the secret bombing of Cambodia and the blanket bombing of Hanoi, at my government's wrongful extension of Manifest Destiny into Southeast Asia? Was there any moral outrage in me at all? No. Despite (or because of) Andy's near-death experiences, Vietnam meant nothing to me except possible death. I never protested. I viewed protesters as privileged college kids with nothing at stake, who, if not exactly getting what they deserved, were fools to place themselves in front of soldiers with loaded weapons and shout obscenities. I was not afforded, nor would I have accepted, the moniker given to my fellow draft refuse-niks who wore their hair long and shouted slogans from the windows of occupied college buildings, that of Conscientious Objector. Where matters of Vietnam were concerned, I had no conscience. I had only the instinct to survive, and that, in the eyes of my government, was not enough.

So after a blurred summer of threats and curses shouted in my face by my father whose voice grew so horse he finally gave way to silence and slapping, and the smoldering contempt of my brother, and Mom's unassuageable weeping, and not one but two visits to our suburban living room by good Pastor Bryant, with his large forehead and pelt of gray hair, who accepted cup after cup of coffee and could not resist the individually-wrapped caramels that were on perpetual display on the coffee table in an ornamental glass candy dish, and who led the family in good Baptist prayers (even Dad who at least sat by silently), and after a visit from my high school counselor, an old man with wet melancholy (rummy) eyes in whose outer office I had spent many an afternoon waiting to be disciplined with yet another term of detention for my latest indiscretion against the behavioral codes of my school (our little dog snarled at him and had to be carried out of the room by Mom), and even after a trip of inquiry to the draft board where a pair of eyeball-to-eyeball officials gave me their Tales of Grim Prison Reality, awkwardly smoking cigarettes and never raising their voices above a menacing whisper, my refusal remained steadfast, and at a pre-arranged time I was arrested by Federal Marshal at my home in the presence of my stoic father and my haggard mother weeping dry-eyed (Andy said his clenched good-byes the night before because, he said, he didn't want to be there to see it), and I was shackled and escorted to a holding facility in Downey, strip-searched and issued an olive drab uniform, then eight days later I was found guilty of a felony and herded with twelve other prisoners into a bus with bars on the windows and an age-old urinous stench rising from the floor boards, and transported for six slow-moving hours to state prison, The Big House, where, with my government's seal of approval, I was deposited in an eleven-by-eight-and-one-half high-ceilinged cinder block cell, in which to remain for two years.

Mira, perhaps your generous nature leads you to envision scenes of me living a martyred imprisonment, writing letters from jail in defense of civil disobedience or some such crap. The truth is, I was not a prisoner of conscience and I did not behave like one. Nor was I treated like one. I was treated like every other inmate, that is, like a stupid, petty criminal, like I'd stolen a pirate-patched Impala and cruised Pacific Coast Highway until I ran a red light and hit a bicyclist, paralyzing him from the waist down; or B&Eed four homes in the same affluent La Jolla neighborhood until I went for a fifth and hit one with an alarm system linked to the police; or held up the same South Gate Rockview drive-in dairy where I'd regularly bought groceries for eight months; or raped a neighborhood girl whose questionable reputation made her appear to me an available object on which to vent frustration; or in a jealous rage stabbed a man repeatedly in the groin with a pocket knife after he'd stolen my girlfriend. These were all crimes of my fellow inmates, told to me by them. My crime was refusal. I was not in their league, and under prison code (which believe me, sweet thing, is stricter even than penal code) I was a nonentity, a prisoner without a pedigree. Mostly I was left alone. Lord knows I was never raped. I was beaten up only once, and that was just a short round of fisticuffs started on the packed-dirt exercise yard by a beetle-browed arsonist with a beard so thin his chin showed through. It's not that he had a fight to pick with me in particular. Maybe he simply hated the smell of me, or just needed to fight. It was broken up by a swarm of guards after they let him spend some heat on me.

For a long time, I sat in my cell wearing a cloak of boredom, picking my nose obsessively. But prison was not a complete waste of time. For one thing, I was put to work in the laundry room. Back home, aside from tossing my dirty clothes in the wicker hamper in the service porch for Mom to deal with, I had never come near laundry. Now I became versed in the humbling trinity of washing-drying-folding.

When the TMers came to the prison at my government's instigation I went through their goofy daisy-strewn ceremony, accepted my own personal secret mantra (eine), and learned to meditate. I meditated in my cell for two months until the inmate across from me took umbrage and began loudly harassing me every time he spotted me sitting on my folding metal chair with my eyes closed. I switched to doing sit-ups on the concrete floor and got as high as 550 in two sets.

I also learned to make the best use of a small space. I learned how to re-direct my sexual energy, and how to discretely spill it in semi-private quarters. And I began to read books, something I obviously had not done in high school. Thereafter,

I remained in a state of delighted astonishment, my nose forever buried in a book. The time passed. I was released.

But I'm afraid I've strayed, haven't I, Mira? Because it doesn't matter what happened to me in prison. At least it doesn't matter tonight as I try to explain why I chose to be sent there in the first place.

The reasons were clear to others at the time. I would not accept the responsibility that comes with adulthood. I would not do my duty by my country. I was selfish. I was a coward. All these were true. But in the years since emerging from prison on a gray and green overcast Sunday morning in September (greeted by my parents who looked at once grim and thankful), I have added one more reason to the list.

In high school there was a guy in the grade ahead of me, Russell Lane, a friend of mine, sort of. He was on the baseball team; played first base. Like the prototypical first baseman, he lacked mobility in the field but could sometimes hit for power. The Dick Stuart of the Norwalk-La Mirada School District. He had a bowl haircut and was gangly and unsure of himself physically. A boy in a man's body. He loved the game.

I sensed that Russell, like me, was still only a partly formed human creature. The next step in life might be the one that mattered most, the one that would shape what kind of man he would be. Russell may not have been old enough or wise enough to take the instruments of self-determination in hand and form his own character.

I know I wasn't. Like most high school kids, he may have been just wondering what would happen next. Life was about to start.

Russell was drafted. He went through basic training at Fort Ord, and before being shipped overseas returned home for a week. Instead of remaining sequestered with his family, Russell, always a self-effacing boy who stayed on the fringe of any circle of friends that would have him, telephoned some old baseball chums and invited them to a good-bye party that he was throwing for himself. I remember it was the first time I'd ever spoken to him on the phone, and when I first heard his excited voice, even though he said his name, I had to think who it could be.

The party took place in his parents' home. It couldn't have been more unlike the socially-debilitated Russell I had known, the Russell who'd been not merely cherry but actually *afraid* to talk with girls. At the front door he greeted everyone (girls included) with an expansive face, a military buzz cut and a handshake. He made sure you had a drink in your hand inside of a minute and spent much of the evening moving through the crowded house with a glass in his hand, laughing, slapping the backs of guys like brothers, flirting with girls.

Russell's parents never made an appearance and after a few hours things got pretty soggy and free-spirited. I remember seeing a guy in his underwear using the living room couch as a trampoline. The music – Stones, Beatles, Cream – pounded out its sweet evasions louder and louder as the night wore on. There were makeout clinches in the dark hall outside the bathroom. Mira, had we been there together that night reveling in our teenage glory I too would have taken you by the hand and gone looking for a dark corner.

In the kitchen was the oddest thing: an overhead florescent light, rigged-up carelessly with wires jutting out and a hole in the ceiling. Its bright sheen gave the room the feel of a school cafeteria. Sometime after midnight a guy vomited on the kitchen floor. The mess, glistening in the florescence, stayed there several minutes before Russell got the poor sick bastard by the ear and stuck his nose in it until he agreed to clean it up. There was no fight. Russell was firm but good-natured about it. I tell you, Mira, that night Russell was not the same shy kid I had slung baseballs to from deep in the hole at short. At times his PFC voice could be heard booming above the music. I saw him dancing with several girls and give them each a long kiss.

Near sunrise, as the party was breaking up, I found myself standing with Russell on the back porch, both of us loaded on Sloe Gin Fizz and Coors (a lethal combination). He was propped flush against the wall, his back rigid, his upward-tilted chin a coarse mix of pinkish acne and sandpaper stubble. I was trying to talk about our days out on the diamond, trying to say admiring things about his long stretch off the bag which saved many an out, and his towering shots to left. But Russell didn't want to talk baseball. There was a look of inflamed confidence in his drunken eyes, of having found his true nature, or, as I suspected, of having been issued his true nature. He looked out at the ripe moon that hung above the garage in the dawn's gathering gray and spoke passionately, if a little slurred, of "greasing gooks." He thrust his beer bottle forward and squinted down the long shaft of his arm as if it were a rifle. Peering into the sights he scanned the backyard for VC. He was looking forward to it. He was sure of himself. "Pow pow pow." He had put away childish things, like baseball, and become a man. I never heard from him and to this day don't know if he came back alive.

So now I've gone and tried to get fancy again, tossing around biblical paraphrases and all. But the point is, Mira, I believed the same would happen to me. My self-will was no greater than Russell's. I believed that I would not be so strong of spine as to keep from bending in the stiff wind of military discipline. I believed that beyond my few idiosyncratic twitches I would become the same kind of man, for the Army demands it.

Naturally, I figured all this out long ago, simple as it is. My simple conclusions resurfaced with renewed clarity since coming to the Land of Milk and Honey; since falling into your arms.

As you say, something is being taken from the young IDF soldiers we see at every turn. And again, I agree. I believe something was taken from me too, my angelic child, as I sat in my cell serving the penalty for my crime. But it wasn't this.
Yours in confession,
Dennis

PAPARAZZI

She is quitting her job and joining the *paparazzi*. She can no longer open the microphone and speak pleasantly (some would say sumptuously) to the cognoscenti about Mozart and museum openings now that the cognoscenti knows what it knows about her broken marriage. "I have a chance to change my life," she tells her dear and loyal friend Johannes as they sup *on Filetti Di Cappone Barcelonette*. They are at Rigoletto's, which was once her favorite restaurant in Little Italy back in the days of marital solidarity, even outright happiness, with Donald. Donald and Debra. Such a dramatic couple they once were. Such animal *chrismo* they generated. Such a socially alert, stylish, vanguard, dramatic couple – now the subject of widespread, albeit whispered, gossip, gossip of the worst kind, gossip confirmed in its most vile and intimate details.

"You can't leave radio, hon," says Johannes, his mouth pushing the words at her. Debra has won Johannes in the breakup despite Donald's stronger ties to their gay friends. In fact, Debra, as the wronged woman, has won most of their friends. Not that Donald, who works fast, hasn't by now cultivated his own impressive new list. "Your presence is too great to be contained by anything less than the airwaves," returns Johannes.

"You're a dear," says Debra. She can tell that Johannes isn't taking her entirely seriously. "But I've already put in my resignation. My last night's Friday."

Johannes, sipping his gibson, is momentarily stunned. He recovers quickly, tuts his tongue, and says with his ever-ready wryness, "I presume that means you'll be leaving Be-more City."

Debra takes the offensive. She has been asked this question countless times once it became clear that Donald, predictably defiant, was staying in Baltimore as artistic director of the opera company and thus forever publicly in her face. "Why is it that *I* should be the one to leave?" she asks.

"You can't be *paparazzi* in this burg, Deb sweetie," returns Johannes, showing genuine concern through his two-cocktail flush. "Who've you got after John Waters?" John Waters, as she and Johannes well know, often frequents Rigoletto's. "You're going to make a career out of taking pictures of John Waters? Get real, hon. The world don't care about our local yokels."

"I'll use Baltimore as a base," says Debra. She hasn't figured it all out yet. "This will be my base and I'll go wherever the pictures take me." It occurs to her that this conversation is the direct inverse of nearly every conversation she has ever had with Johannes. He's always been the one detailing *his* plans for the future, *his* schemes for love-lorn revenge, *his* heart-thrummings for a new squeeze, not vice versa.

"And what are you going to live on," says Johannes, flourishing his non-eating hand, "while you find your way, I mean, you know, while you learn the business?"

Leaning forward, propping her chin on her palm, she smiles and says, "Maryland has such wonderful laws." She has told herself that on principle she is against living off Donald's money. But she'll take advantage of the situation for a while if she has to.

The *Filetti Di Cappone Barcelonette* is *eccellente*. She rolls a morsel of chicken and a mushroom around in her mouth. Food hasn't tasted of anything for a long time. It even occurred to her that maybe her taste buds soured along with her heart. In three months, she's lost twenty-five pounds, fifteen of which she could ill-afford to lose. Last week Johannes even took her aside and with painful, drunken honesty in his eyes asked her straight away if maybe she didn't think she was inching a bit too close to anorexia. He had friends who'd exhibited the same signs. He was worried for her and wanted her to see a doctor he knew. They both knew he wasn't really worried about anorexia, but that other A. No, answered Debra, she wasn't anorexic, just divorced, or on her way. But now with this new inspiration, with this new hope on the horizon, with something interesting to look forward to besides fornicating vengefully and indiscriminately, maybe some of life's simple pleasures were returning to her. She hoped so with all her heart. Who would have thought that chicken could be life-affirming?

"Deb sweetie," says Johannes, who has seen her act too impulsively for her own good a few times before. "I wouldn't want to rain on your ambitions. I want to just say `Go for it, hon, giv'em what for,' but I don't think it hurts to really ask yourself the hard questions. Like for instance, do you know the first thing about taking pictures?"

Debra knows what he means, but she feels she possesses qualities that are more important to being part of the *paparazzi* than knowing the ins and outs of the camera and its accessories. First of all, she knows what it means to be famous, since she is herself famous, at least locally. People recognize her. She's ridden in parades, made countless public appearances at record stores, neighborhood ethnic festivals, and malls. She's been profiled often in local mags and papers. Criminy, she's on the radio five nights a week. She knows what it's like to be approached in restaurants by people asking for autographs, sometimes even with cameras. And because she has been one herself and believes that fame is fame varying only by degrees, she knows how to approach famous people, and this will help her immeasurably in getting pictures. But even more importantly, she believes she carries within her the requisite mix of fascination and contempt for famous people that will allow her to hunt them down and take their picture. The hunt – that will be the thrill of the job. It will hold her interest, at least until she finds something better to do. But she cannot say these things to Johannes. He would take it the wrong way. So instead she says, "What's to know?"

*

In fact, Debra *does* know something about taking pictures. Two years ago, she bought a Nikon N2000 that the camera salesman, a venerable Dutch uncle of a gentleman who genuinely seemed to have her interests at heart, called "a serviceable camera for the serious amateur." She has taken a Johns Hopkins continuing studies class and done some serious amateur photography – not only still lifes of tulips in Sherwood Gardens, but portraits of friends, culminating in a stunning series of ten B&Ws of Donald, nude, dancing.

Donald was congenitally attentive to his body, but Debra made him look even more sensational; a great-mane Adonis. She hung the photos in the upstairs hallway outside their bedroom. Many of their friends commented on these portraits, not simply amused that Donald should display himself so (that was no news), but admiring the craftsmanship – artistry, really – of Debra's work.

Donald dancing. Whenever she thinks of those pictures she huffs bitterly at the irony. Donald's dancing was the start of it. "All dancing is about fucking," Donald once told her during their early days together at St. John's. There in the Great Books program Donald's special interest was world religions; Debra's modern languages. He instructed her in the ways of Brahmanism, she tutored him in Italian, and together they learned the strange animal travesty of dancing. They would ballroom dance at Naval Academy dress-white affairs, posing for pictures with midshipmen, then still formally garbed they ran into the Annapolis night to a leathery bar eight steps below the sidewalk, jammed hip-to-hip with sweating queers and criminals, and dance until, as Donald said, they became like Gran Chaco Indians – no religion, no idolatries, no distinctions of moral and immoral, no thought of assuaging the wrath of a supernatural power. Donald had a favorite pair of black Armani pants that flattered the long curves of his ass and set his crouch in bold relief. At the end of the long night they would compare notes as to who got groped more on the dance floor. Donald usually won.

They fell in love. She gave herself to him more than she believed she would ever give herself to a man. Ever since she was a girl she had taken pride in her independence of thought and maintained a wary, if appreciative, eye for the opposite sex. But Donald was an open book of honest intellect and passion. He concealed nothing, and thereby allowed her to do the same with him. He was also an intoxicating combination of debauchery and tenderness, of haughty disdain for pretension and humility in the face of his betters. One minute he'd be playfully spanking her amid a torrent of misogynist obscenities, and the next he'd be on his knees before her chanting a Hopi prayer of worship. She decided that what she had with Donald was what was meant by *soulmates*. They were married while still at school.

By the time they moved up to Baltimore to make their foray into the arts – she as midday announcer at the classical music station, he as assistant to the opera's executive director – Debra had sweated out much of her dance fever. Forty-five minutes on the dance floor and she was drained, not so much physically exhausted as weary of motion. Sometimes dancing seemed like nothing but monotonously bobbing up and down, repeating the same moves moronically over and over. She would drop her hands, give Donald a pooped smile, and go back to their table to cool down and comb out the sweaty kinks in her hair. Donald was left to shake his shock of wavy orange locks with whoever had the energy – or more than energy, the courage – to take him up on his howling come-on to dance.

"I have," said Donald, "a pash to mash." What's more, after a few years Donald's presence in Baltimore began to grow, due in no small measure, he said, to the business he conducted on the dance floor. Debra began to get rides home with friends, leaving Donald to dance another couple of hours. Then her shift at the station was switched to weeknights and she had an excuse not to go at all, though sometimes he persuaded her to call in sick.

In hindsight she has wondered if she should have seen it coming. But, how could she? They had a solid marriage built on trust and the freedom to do what they wished without having to account for every minute they were apart. Things were so good between them she had even begun to think about the unthinkable: children. Besides that, Donald's choice of a regular dance mate was perfect for everyone involved: Max. Max, high-strung and ultra-hip, was a key player at the Baltimore Foundation, the city's chief distributor of grant monies to the arts. She was also a dear friend to both Debra and Donald and would no more betray one than the other. Max was even in need of a dance partner herself. Her lover, Moira, didn't dance, owning less to a lack of pash than to a hairline crack in a lumbar vertebra.

At first Debra didn't believe stories from friends about Donald and Max's hot display – or lurid public spectacle – in Fells Point clubs. She considered it all mean-spirited fun; not so untypical of her friends. She refused, on principle, to confront Donald. She understood how business was done. Besides that, Donald showed not the slightest sign that his affections had wandered. Not the slightest.

But the stories continued. According to friends, Donald and Max had not simply formed an intimate alliance of arts institutions, but were into a romance of the serious kind, the total sweaty, hip-churning, groin-spasm package. So the night it happened, Debra though in hindsight, was it really such a great surprise?

At the station, Debra spent all day putting her program on D.A.T., then during her shift, at her legal peril, she left the station. She came home to find the stereo downstairs loudly playing the Haydn *Divertimento* that in the car she'd just heard herself introduce. Upstairs all the lights were on and the door to the guest bedroom was wide open. When she first heard his moans she thought, hopefully, he was masturbating. *What fun, I'll break in on him jerking off.* She knew he would enjoy that and invite her to finish the job. But by the time she got halfway down the hall she heard two moans of filthy carnal excitement. In the doorway, she saw the truth: Donald and Max, narcotized, *in flagrante delicto di flagrante peccato*. They were much too involved to notice her. Max was on her knees doing jaw exercises. Donald was draped back across the bed, wearing Debra's own peach silk charmeuse camisole.

Rather than bursting in, Debra stood a moment trying to catch her breath. She gathered enough presence of mind to turn around, walk down the hall, passing the dancing Donald photos, and go to the bedroom. She might have retrieved the small black pistol that Donald kept in the bottom of the armoire. The option was in the air for a moment. "Not a jury in the land," she later said to her dearest friends before thinking that her dearest friends would quickly tell their dearest friends.

Instead she retrieved her N2000, crept back down the hall, and walked boldly into the guest bedroom, camera clicking.

Next day, sleepless and shaken, Debra was in the darkroom of her friend Peter, watching as her divorce evidence materialized in the sink before her. "Publishable quality," smirked Peter as he hung the prints from a clothesline. "A case of grace under pressure." Debra leaned over the sink to get a better look, and Peter gave her an unambiguous ass grab. She waited until they finished developing the entire roll and she had the pictures in her hand before she rebuked him with a whopping, Stanwickesque slap in the face.

Donald filled two suitcases and without a word of repentance (as if this was something he expected her to learn to live with and make it snappy), took up temporary residence at the Belvedere, walking distance from the opera offices. Debra assumed responsibility for distributing the hurt equally by performing the heartbreaking chore of informing Moira of her lover's gross indiscretion. Moira was an innocent, moon-faced, pasta-cooking child, who seemed to want little more in life than Max's motherly breasts to suckle. Debra thought about it throughout an entire shift, then decided she didn't give a damn who got hurt and mailed Moira a choice 5X7 color shot showing Max g'd up and greedily gnawing the antithesis of her militantly avowed sexual preference. "Imagine the poor child opening the envelope," Debra speculated to her dearest friends.

Within a week Donald's illness brought him home and laid him flat on his back in the very bed in which he and Max. ...It was hepatitis C. It overwhelmed Donald. He couldn't even walk. Debra had to help him out of bed and into the bathroom, and every third day she supported him on her shoulders as they went from the parking lot to the Dr. Pickins's office for an injection of interferon. "Hepatitis C is usually transmitted through sexual activity," the doctor told them both.

"No kidding," said Debra.

"I say that as a warning, not as a judgment," said Dr. Pickins.

"Yeah, well," said Debra.

Dr. Pickins's warning to Donald was to get complete rest, eat well, and that a side effect of the interferon could be some moderate hair loss. Each morning as she brought Donald breakfast, averting her eyes as she passed the series of B&Ws in the hall, Debra hoped to see huge orange fistsful of hair on his pillow. She stole glances at his hairline. If he's losing hair he's concealing it, she thought. Anyway, Donald's mane was great enough that a few missing fistfuls wouldn't show.

He relied on Debra to wait on him hand and foot, and she, unable to abandon him in his hour of greatest need any more than she could abandon a wounded dog, *did* wait on him hand and foot. Swollen with hatred, Debra made one condition: "You're not to communicate with your slit-slavering friend." She drew close to his face, so he could feel the heat of her rage; could see the dark, soggy stains beneath her eyes. "You're not to talk to her on the phone. She's not to come near this house."

"Don't worry," said Donald. "She has her own problems. As you well know."

Three times Debra caught him sneaking phone calls to Max. She just couldn't bring herself to throw him out.

Naturally, the house was stormed by friends and opera folk, come to proffer their flowers and good wishes for a fast recovery. Donald, lying abed, engulfed in a floral sea and buoyed by six down pillows, with books, note pads, and telephone by his side, greeted everyone as usual: urbane, affable, a fireproof smile. But his brushed-back hair revealed a patina of jaundiced yellow at the edges of his face, and he could meet for no more than a few minutes before he was drained and stranded in a silence of vast indifference. Upon the departure of each guest Donald called Debra to the room so he could give her his capsule review, as part of his shameless efforts to thaw the ice around Debra's heart. There was the mezzo from Pittsburgh. "She's built her sputtering, libidinous career on Carmen," said Donald. "Now the little ingenue's forty-six and her Carmen's no more sexy than cottage cheese." There was the local tenor who years ago had gone to New York with Heldenian dreams, blown out his vocal cords on *Gotterdammerung*, and last year returned to Baltimore thankful for the chance to sing the harlequin in Donald's off-beat (but exciting) *Pagliacci*. There was the suave Latino conductor of past promise who'd made a disastrous career move by leaving his assistant conductorship with a front rank European chamber orchestra to become music director of a third-tier Midwest symphony, only to watch in horror as a financial scandal erupted on the board of directors, which led to the city withdrawing its support, which led to the symphony crashing and burning. "He wants to climb back up the ladder on my rungs," said Donald.

One afternoon Debra was at the kitchen table with the bottle of Veuve Clicquot Ponsardin that Johannes had given them last Christmas. She'd popped it open after Johannes arrived to visit Donald, with the intent of showing Johannes that she was no longer saving it for a special occasion. She had *Traveler* open before her and was trying to concentrate on an article about the Japanese hot spring, *onsen* (*To understand the Japanese, there is only one True Way: You must bathe with them*). From upstairs she heard Donald signal with his small mammy bell – a clear, high-pitched copper bell made to look like a black mammy in a calico dress, a souvenir from a vacation that had taken them plantation hopping through Virginia and the Carolinas. She had been half-expecting to hear the bell. Donald didn't really like Johannes. "Between thee and me," Donald once told her, "I think we'll one day find ourselves delivering lunches and fresh sheets to our pretty friend's flat." Debra sipped the wine and ignored the bell. She was reading a paragraph about Buddhism. Being famous among friends for her compulsive marginalia, she jotted in the margin: *Typical god-deluded mumbo jumbo.* She and Donald had planned to travel one day to the Orient. That's not going to happen now, she thought. Minutes later Donald again rang the mammy bell, this time a little more insistently. Eventually she went upstairs.

The room smelled richly of flowers and Donald's cologne, not a sick room at all. Donald was saying to Johannes that at the very least he was lucky he'd fallen ill now and not in the middle of the season, though of course now his summer travel plans were in jeopardy. He stopped in mid-sentence when he saw Debra in the doorway. A spark of perturbation flashed in his brandy eyes. Donald could never abide being made to wait.

"What is it?" said Debra in a voice so cold it turned the back of Johannes' neck pink. Johannes of course knew all about the story behind Donald's hepatitis. When Debra had brought him upstairs he'd nodded meaningfully as they passed the hallway, gravely noting the B&W portraits of Donald.

Johannes turned in the chair and greeted Debra with a look of tartuffery, as if this were a mock death-watch over the Pope. Debra nearly burst out laughing despite herself. Dear Johannes was trying to remain neutral, knowing that many a marriage has survived adultery.

Not that this was going to be one of them.

"Darling," said Donald, his lips greasy with ersatz affection, "would you mind please getting me my eye drops from the master bathroom?"

Getting me my eye drops was the code phrase Donald had devised that meant he wanted her to graciously expedite the swift exit of his present visitor. Debra thought this little cowardly game of his was pathetic. It was cowardly play-acting, and it exemplified the degradation that Donald's once broad and open honesty had suffered. Yet, she had dutifully carried out his game four times in the last week alone. Donald said he had a perfectly sound reason for it. He didn't think it smart politically to be telling well-meaning and perhaps useful guests to leave. A conspiratorial smile crossed his lips as he added that by pretending to be in need of eye drops he could also close his eyes and no longer have to look upon the person he wished gone.

Debra stood in the doorway looking at Donald with a detachment that felt foreign. *Betraying no emotion*, she thought, the way defendants are described in the newspaper as they listen to the judge sentence them. Should she go through this charade again, and with Johannes yet? Not only was Johannes her dear friend, but he was much too skilled in the ways of social deception to be fooled by such a rank, transparent ruse. She could always shoo Johannes out and apologize later.

"Did Donald tell you the hepatitis is causing him to lose his hair?" said Debra. Yes, that was good. Plant the rumor right before Donald's eyes.

Johannes, his chin tilted significantly upward, turned to Donald for confirmation.

"No," said Donald. His brow furrowed. He looked to Johannes then to Debra then to Johannes. "They said it *might*, a little, but it hasn't. See."

"How awful for you," said Johannes. Then, trying to crack the tension, he added, "Get Christian, hon. From now on there are some naughties you are going to have to do without."

Debra slipped out of the room. What was *that*? she thought. Some kind of no-secrets-among-chums gesture? Thank you, no.

She passed through her bedroom. It was *her* bedroom now, not theirs, and she'd let it grow wild with strewn clothes. She paused at the armoire for a moment of malicious amusement, stooping, opening a drawer and withdrawing Donald's four-inch black pistol. It looked like smooth black glass and fit perfectly in her slender hand. It weighed only about as much as a telephone receiver. Not much for a gun, she thought. It would probably weigh a lot more if it were loaded. She knew how to load it too. Donald had shown her. Then, as she looked at the pistol, a black, coagulated taste formed in the back of her mouth and the malicious amusement soured to disgust – at herself; at Donald for turning her into a monster who daydreams of shooting her husband in his sick bed.

She put the pistol away, got the eye drops, and went back to Donald's bedroom. By then she'd decided not to graciously suggest to Johannes that he should be leaving because Donald needed his rest. She didn't want to go through the routine of fighting off Donald's feigned objections. She didn't want to have to evoke the name of Dr. Pickins and quote his instructions. She would no longer play Donald's pathetic, repugnant game. Instead, she put the eye drops on the table next to Donald's bed and left without a word or eye contact, leaving Donald to fend for himself.

In the mail that day was the St. John's *Alumni Magazine*. She flipped to the Class Notes section. Among the long lists of tiny-typeface announcements of alumni job promotions, marriages, deaths, etc., was a blank form: WHAT NEWS HAVE YOU? She tore out the form and put it in her handbag. That evening at work, during the Beethoven Symphony No.1, she filled it out.

Donald Woodwell. Deceased. Auto accident, April 29. Survived by his wife, Debra Infante.

She listed herself as the contact. Two weeks later, when a woman from the St. John's *Alumni Magazine* called to confirm the news, Debra answered: "Yes."

*

First there is the matter of equipment. Early one sunny Saturday, she returns to the camera shop where she bought her N2000. She asks for the venerable Dutch uncle of a gentleman with whom she dealt two years ago. She has no trouble remembering his name. He owns the store: Taube's Photo.

This time Taube knows her from the radio. He says he listens at home. He asks what kind of photography she'll be doing. She does not hesitate in answering, "*Paparazzi*." She has wondered if a serious photographer like himself would disapprove.

But Taube does not disapprove. "Then you'll certainly be needing a zoom," he says.

"Money is no issue," says Debra. "Consider yourself Pygmalion for a day."

Taube eyes her carefully. "And a telephoto," he says, then turns and vanishes into the stock room. Moments later he returns with a Sigma 90mm F2.8 zoom. The lens is only two-and-a-half inches but weighs, she is amused to think, about the same as Donald's pistol. Taube says it will bring her subject from across the street "up close and personal." Debra isn't sure if he's mocking her.

Next, Taube shows her a telephoto, a massive Celestron C90 with a scope mounted on top. He says that from a roof she'll be able to zero in on celebrities a half-mile away. He has a mischievous lilt in his voice. "You'll need a tripod."

"Won't I need a better camera?" says Debra.

"Your Nikon will do fine," says Taube.

"It's got to be the professional best."

"It's not the camera that matters," says Taube. "It's the lens. And the photographer."

"I want everything that's needed," she says.

Next comes a strange looking flash: a light-ring, the shape of a baby toilet seat. Taube says, "It'll keep you flashing all night out in front of a swank restaurant." There's a light meter, a leather camera case, and a large travelling case lined with thick, unyielding foam padding.

"You're developing your own?" asks Taube.

"I can't imagine who else would," says Debra.

So Taube leads her into the bright and well-ordered stock room, where he picks out and explains the darkroom supplies she will need: orange lights and tanks and drums and racks and chemicals. She had no idea there was so much involved, down to lintless cotton gloves and a vinyl apron. Finally, there are stacks of polycontrast paper, B&W and color.

They spend five hours together, concluding at two-thirty with lunch, Debra's treat. Lunch is three blocks away in a crowded and clamorous Italian restaurant. Taube has sloped shoulders and a diaphanous ring of hair around his pinkish, age-flecked skull. His venerableness, it seems to Debra, is not merely a veneer. In her eyes he has traveled long and familiarly in the brooding moral hinterlands. It's nothing he's said exactly. Just a look he has. But then during the meal he becomes giddy as a pooch. Giddy from being in her presence. He eats in spurts.

Debra knows her beauty. Her hair may be skinned back to look severe, and she may be several pounds below her ideal weight, but she knows she is blessed with a fine, ample nose and dark, hooded eyes – a Raphael Madonna. She knows too that much of her beauty comes from her manner of unceasing forward momentum. She leans over the table with languid arrogance as she speaks. She imagines that someone watching from across the restaurant would think that she and Taube were carrying on a May-December affair. She wants to tell Taube her whole sorry story, but also doesn't want to. It is indeed a sunny and preparatory day.

"Today you are my most trusted friend," says Debra.

Taube is ready with a quip: "Then trust that you are now equipped to hunt down whatever you're after."

"Loaded for bear?" flirts Debra.

Taube snickers. "Loaded for bear."

She wonders if she has fallen in love with this venerable Dutch uncle of a gentleman. If he were twenty years younger, she thinks, she would take him home and do with him what she has done with many men in the last few months, except in the case of her dear friend Mr. Taube, with tenderness. *Ten* years younger.

Taube says he will arrange for everything to be delivered to her house tomorrow. She kisses him on the cheek good-bye. "Send me your first sale," says Taube.

*

Friday comes, and Debra blows off her final air shift. She needs this day for travel. She has already received her first tip. Johannes heard from his new flame, Fabian, who heard from Donald, whose sources are impeccable, that opera's heir apparent to Pavarotti, a three-octave Italian tenor with presence in the historic manner and androgynous *bellezza*, is rendezvousing at a spa in California at some place called Borrego Springs with the hottest new American soprano, a twenty-three-year-old wide-eyed delight of Wisconsin purity, who has scored at the Met and Santa Fe and recently leapt into the mainstream press with her Grammy CD of twenties art songs. She made *Esquire's* "Register." *People* reports she is married to her soulmate from Juilliard, whose own career is evolving nicely as first violinist of the quartet-in-residence at Duke. The happy couple are expecting their first child in two months.

Debra feels she knows all these people. So often she has said their records on the radio.

She calls an editor at *Celeb Search*, a tabloid with lots of color. Surely, she thought, color meant money. She's glad the editor is a woman, J.B. Keller. The editor says she'll look at pictures if Debra can get them, no promises, no expenses.

"You're a novice, honey," says the editor.

Debra flies to LAX, rents a car and takes off for Anza-Borrego Desert. Three hours later she's entering the valley, descending the side of a brown mountain, and a wave of heat hits her full in the face, like a hot blast from the oven felt when she used to bake for Donald...stop it, she told herself, she wasn't going into all that mother-fuckin' shit right now. The landscape is strictly gray brush. She's never felt heat like this. Feels good in her skin.

The town, Borrego Springs, is hardly your glitterati resort. There is a short main drag of hardware stores and polyester shops. Everything looks closed for the summer, except for a grocery/general store. Beyond the main strip there are small clusters of mobile homes, aluminum ghost towns. Sweating in the seat, she circles wide but finds no sign of a spa, and she's about to start another sweep when suddenly she sees a bright green strip of grass jutting out from gray brush at the roadside. It's no more than six feet. She gets out to examine. She peers through a gray hedge. It's the edge of a golf course. "Where there's golf, there's a spa," she says.

But after driving around in large dusty circles, then stopping at the grocery store for directions (the checker shrugged indifferently, he didn't know), then driving in more large dusty circles, her thighs clenching a sweaty bottle of Gatorade, Debra is still nowhere. Then, way up a narrow incline, maybe three hundred feet, she spots a foot-square hand-written sign stuck in the gravel embankment: Kit Fox Spa. She walks up the incline and finds a stone fence entrance sequestered in a palm oasis. She wonders how people drive their cars in here. Approaching the entrance, she becomes more conscious of how she looks – halter and shorts, the embroidered strap of her N2000 slung over her shoulder. Suddenly, like an awakening, she sees she should have had some way to conceal the camera. Already she feels like she's in over her head.

A guard in khaki uniform and pith helmet watches motionlessly from within a cone-top tiki hut. Her only chance, she thinks, is her pious and sweat-drenched beauty. She'll pretend to be lost. She removes her midnight sunglasses, so the guard can see her innocent, questioning eyes. But the look in the guard's eyes could puncture her skin. No way is she getting in here. I have failed before I've even begun, thinks Debra.

The guard's face is sun-dashed Egyptian brown. He would be handsome but for his squashed nose and the hard suspicion in his eyes.

Abandoning her pretense, Debra says, "What must I have to get in?"

"Today you win the Lotto, *paparazzi*," says the guard, grimacing from beneath the broad brim of his pith helmet. His voice is surprisingly tender-throated; almost a boy's. "I'm quitting this job."

Debra nudges forward. "You mean you'll let me in?"

"I mean I'm going back to Duquesne."

"I know people in Pittsburgh." She almost starts to say, "I was Catholic once," but catches herself. "Thank you."

He pauses to grimace at her. "It costs."

Debra figures she knows the cost, and she's prepared to pay it. This is no time to hesitate. "You

think we can manage standing up in your little tiki?"
She moves closer to him, her sweaty self in his aura.

"Keep it covered, *paparazzi*. You people are diseased."

"Then *what*, money? I can't do that. Not as a journalist?"

"Five hundred."

Debra looks away and does a quick mental sum of ready funds. The equipment and the plane ticket have nearly cleaned her out. She looks past the guard. Tapering away from the entrance, the stone fence is topped by barbed wire. "I'm going to have to get it," she says. "But first, tell me, are they in there?"

"The fee," says the guard.

Debra returns to the main drag and finds a cramped store-front pizza joint that's open. She's the only customer. She thinks about buying wire cutters tomorrow and climbing the fence. But she knows she won't. She checks into the Hacienda del Sol motel. Hers is the only car in the parking lot. The room reeks of bug poison. Leaning against the doorjamb, she watches the solemn sky fading to black. The quiet is etched at the edges by rodents scurrying and cawing black birds flying over the roofs of empty motel rooms.

It's after one back in Baltimore, she thinks. She calls Johannes. There is music and noise in the background. She imagines a living room of half-naked dancing fags. Johannes is high'd up. She has a hard time getting him to understand her.

"I said I need five hundred dollars to get in," says Debra. "Can you wire me five hundred dollars?"

"Five hundred?" says Johannes. "For what? You paying them to pose?"

"Listen, please. I said I-need-the-money-to-get-in."

"I hear you just fine, hon. You need to bribe the guard to get in. I gotch'ya. So why not sneak in? Climb a fence. That's the way the pros do it."

"You don't know what it's like here," says Debra. "There's barbed wire. I'm sure there's dogs. I'll pay you back."

"A what?" Johannes is speaking to someone else in the room. Then back to Debra: "Oh, excellent. Rent a hot air balloon! How's that, Deb sweetie? And tell me, you ever do it in a hot air balloon? Up up and away!"

"Are you going to help me or not?"

"Deb Sweetie, you know I love you, and if I had the money I'd give it to you in a second, but you also have to know that I *do not* walk around with money like that in my pocket. I'm month to month. Why don't you try Donald?"

Debra, sitting on the edge of the bed in a dark, sweaty room at the Hacienda del Sol motel, puts the receiver in her lap. She shouldn't have called. Her first obstacle and she can't function. She's about to hang up, but Johannes is shouting into the phone.

"Look, here's an idea! Why not check in?"

"Great idea," Debra sneers. "And what's that going to cost, three times the amount? Don't worry about it, I'll figure it out. Good bye, dear."

"Nonono, don't hang up! We got the blueprint right here. We've got it, we do. Here's what we do. First, I go over to your house and make a few calls to friends far away. You can use your phone bill as your alibi that you were home. You can call your super to let me in. He knows me. Next, you call in your reservation to the spa. Say that you're coming in from LA tomorrow, for a week. Are you writing this down, Deb my sweet?"

"Go ahead."

"Ok, tomorrow you show up at the spa all covered up and done over and mysterious. So they can't recognize you absolutely later. You flash your VISA and do your *paparazzi* thing. Then you scram out of there, get home, and discover, oh my god, someone has stolen your VISA. She called it in right away. Your phone bill will help you cover your ass, if it comes to that. And anyway, Sammy and I will vouch for you that you were here the whole time."

"I'm not following all this with the phone bill and everything."

"All right, here's the scenario. First, somebody stole your card. They used it to fly to LA, then used it at the spa. *Semplice*. It's worth a try, yes?"

"I don't know."

"What's the worst that could happen?"

"I'll think about it. There's got to be holes in that."

"Deb, lamb chop, baby cakes! We'll all pulling for you here! Remember, the great ones do what it takes!"

"I don't know."

"*Vanity Fair* is calling you!"

Debra laughs.

"Giv'em what for!"

"Who's Sammy?" asks Debra.

"Who's *Sammy*!" exclaims Johannes.

Next morning the heat slams onto the motel room like a flat rock. Debra makes herself up grotesquely, especially around her eyes with gobs of eye shadow and wide streaks of eyebrow pencil. She rats her hair wildly. She laughs at herself in the mirror. After breakfast at the town coffee shop, where a pair of ham and eggers in baseball caps eye her with sleepy lust and the flustered waitress asks what she means by "*iced* coffee," Debra is again standing at the stone fence entrance to the Kit Fox Spa, this time with a reservation.

"You've double-crossed me, *paparazzi*," says the guard, emerging from his cone-top tiki hut. His eyes are submerged in deep morning shadow from the brim of his pith helmet. "I can turn you in."

"You can," Debra says, stepping forward. "Here, I brought you a little something. Something between us Catholics." She gives him an envelope containing seventy dollars. "For text books at Duquesne." She kisses him hard on the lips.

"I should have banged you when I had the chance," says the guard.

"Think of it this way," says Debra. "How much do you hate them?"

"It's true. I hate all of them, all the world."

"All the world will see these pictures."

"Go with grace, *paparazzi*," says the guard. "The Diva and Divo take their jacuzzi at six. Get out alive."

All the suites, magnificent as Medici tombs, open onto a grassy, trapezoid piazza. The walkway that halves the piazza is edged with terra-cotta pots overflowing with geraniums and impatiens. The gently rising grassy oval mound climaxes in an icy blue jacuzzi big enough to accommodate thirty in luxury. From her upstairs dormer window Debra has a panoramic view of all the action. A desert *passeggiata*, she thinks.

She stakes out her tripod at the window and mounts her N2000 with the telephoto. Peering into the scope, she can make out tiny fissures in the sky-blue tile around the rim of the jacuzzi.

While she's here, she thinks, it's a shame not to sample some of the spa's opulence. She could go for a long, sulfurous mud facial, or the sassafras-oiled hands of a sage masseur, or a green seaweed paste body wrap, or one of the finely made young concierges in white linen sleeveless tunics. But she is compelled to remain stationed at her post, a job to do. Lounging on the bed against a heap of Porthault pillows, staring out into the midday glare, Debra observes as russet and perspiring patrons, mostly women, come and go. They approach the jacuzzi with the suppliant reverence of pilgrims at a shrine. They shed their loose-fitting garments and leave them draped over the peach chintz armchairs. Submerged to the collarbone in the bubbling water, the patrons sip Evian or sunset-colored drinks served them by deferential, dark-skinned Kit Fox servants. Debra reminds herself again that she is not here to play. There is still no sign of her prey. To pass the time she seeks the surest succor of her own slender fingers. They have been her steadfast friends throughout these last terrible months. They make her groan in approval.

A few minutes after six, the Divo appears from behind a white neo-Corinthian column, his charmed and famous smile uplifted to the bravoing sun, his features disarmingly exquisite, his coiled hair black as the devil's heart. He moves as if invested with the ponderous secrets of the Milky Way, and yet clearly, he is glad and winsome with the broad expanse of his life. No wonder this man sings so of love and death, Debra thinks, her heart pumping fierce Gran Chaco rhythms. He makes Donald look like a wind-up toy. She swings the camera on its tripod and snaps four shots directly at the great tenor's unrestrained and caramel chest.

Seconds later the Diva emerges in his wake, out of the shadows of the portico. She is abundantly pregnant in a bikini yet carrying her bronze mound before her with ancient Roman virtue.

Voyeurs   DJB

Together they walk across the grassy piazza toward the jacuzzi, not hand-in-hand but with the tender familiarity that comes of new love.

Debra is breathless at her luck. At the jacuzzi's edge the Divo steps out of his swim trunks, revealing no tan lines and a magnificence that makes Debra cluck incoherently.

The Diva steps gingerly into the jacuzzi and sits on a step, submerged only to the middle of her great swelled dome. She leans her head back to face the sun. The Divo dunks himself and comes up beside his giggling American mistress. He palms water onto her stomach and watches with the fascination of a child as it runnels off in all directions. He hooks his arm over her, as if it were *his* bambino whose womb he was cradling. He cooingly smooches her navel with his full, famous, guileless lips. Debra's hands are trembling. The tripod has saved her. Each click and whir of the N2000 sounds loud and sweet.

By the next morning she has driven back to L.A., flown home, developed her film, and Fed Exed the ten best shots to the editor at *Celeb Search*, who buys them at nine the next morning over the phone for $8,200. Debra is certain that's low-dollar because she's a novice. *The Celeb Search* editor says, "Opera is fringe for us."

Then the *Celeb Search* editor tells her, "You show good chops, Ms. Infante." She wants to see more work. "How often do you get to the city?"

A week later a three-photo spread appears on page 17, complete with a story based loosely on the things Debra told the editor. SHOCKING DECADENCE! OPERA GIANT AND PREGNANT SINGER CAVORT ON SLY AT EXCLUSIVE SPA! *Husband home preparing nursery*. Debra sends a copy to Taube with a note: "The first bear, he hath been bagged."

Thus, her new career is under way. One night she waits outside Rigoletto's for two hours and gets a shot of John Waters coming out. The editor at *Celeb Search* takes it for $450, but the picture does not run.

She receives e-mail from the *Celeb Search* editor telling her about a celebrity charity basketball game that's to take place that night at a high school gymnasium in New York, and she stands in her first *paparazzi* line. There's no jostling for position like she envisioned. About a dozen *paparazzi* wait outside the entrance and shoot TV and sports celebs as they slowly make their way from limo to gymnasium. Nobody says much. Everyone's there on a job. Debra feels almost invisible behind her camera, though she does notice one man in the line, a pale, fleshy face, occasionally watching her with undisguised desire. Once all the celebs have come and gone and the *paparazzi* begin to disperse, this man approaches her. She's not in the mood to be hit on, but she's anxious to see up close the kind of people who work in her newly chosen profession.

"You're new, aren't you?" the man says, coming on like a sportscaster.

"Not really."

"Yes you are. I can tell. I know everyone out here."

"A real veteran, eh?"

"Art Buist," he says, sticking out his hand as if she has been waiting in line to meet him. Even at arm's length his breath is foul. He is a large-boned man with hair at his temples matted in sweaty rings. His eyelids are pinkish as a laboratory mouse. He seems good enough natured in a dull-witted sort of way, thinks Debra. He's probably very workman-like – standing around on sidewalks taking routine celebrity photos. Maybe not someone who's going to go after a hot air balloon shot, or for that matter not someone likely to pull off something like her Borrego caper. But he probably gets the job done day after day.

"Well, Art Buist," says Debra, shaking his sweaty hand, "who do you work for?"

"Boy oh boy, you *are* new?"

Debra, caught unaware, goes immediately on the offensive. "What's that supposed to mean?"

"It means that I work for who pays me, like everyone out here."

She likes this man less with every second. Blunt, stupid, an arrested adolescent. His wet mouth hangs flaccidly ajar. His breath stinks. Boy oh boy? "Is that right," she says, salting her voice with disdain.

"Yeah that's right. Let me tell you something," says Art Buist. He sucks his teeth. "I'm as good as they get out here. Let me tell you. I can tell you some things to get you started off on the right foot. So you don't fall all over yourself. Let me tell you. Here's your first lesson. Are you ready for your first lesson? The number one rule out here is this. Touch someone else's camera and die. You keep that in mind and you can't go too far wrong."

"Did I touch your camera, Art Buist?"

"Be a smart ass if you want, but if you're going to be out here you'll see. I can tell you a lot. I'm as good as they get. Come and have a drink with me and I'll tell you some things."

"I have to be going."

"No you don't. Where do you have to go? The shoot's over. Come and have a drink. There's a place I know that's right down the street."

"Are you always this presumptuous?"

"Look, new girl, if you want to work this racket you have to know people. You have to be out among the people. Talk to the people. Come and have a drink."

"No. Is that clear enough, Mr. Buist? No."

"Next time then. You'll see me next time."

Two days later, the *Celeb Search* editor buys two shots of a Soap Hunk that Debra had never in her life seen until the instant when everyone else in the *paparazzi* line turned their cameras his way and she did the same. She gets $950. Like most photos in the magazine, hers run without a credit.

Johannes knows the Soap Hunk. He's a fan. "He's engaged in holy bedlock with the grieving, and filthy rich young widow Mrs. Bross," Johannes informs Debra as they lunch at a sidewalk table outside Henry and Jeff's. "I take it then you're finding the gossip biz suited to your temperament."

"It's easier than I thought it would be," says Debra.

"What's the best part, hon? Rubbing tushes with the rich and famous?"

She doesn't have an answer to this, though admittedly she has tried not to think about it too much. Recently she read an article about the rise of *paparazzi* which quoted one of Donald's old professors at St. John's. She remembers Donald describing this Prof. as a brilliant theoretician who didn't hold too strong a grasp on the real world. "An egghead with a thin shell." It's the revenge factor, the Prof. was quoted. Celebrities are made to pay for their success by suffering public humiliation when things go wrong in their private lives. It's a theory, thinks Debra, as good as any other.

"I don't know what I like about it actually," she tells Johannes, who suddenly doesn't seem all that interested. His fingers are drawing patterns in the moisture on his wine glass. Johannes is a brilliant social deceiver, but with her he never tries to fake it when he's bored. It's one of his endearing qualities. "I guess the money's good," she says dismissively. "I'll say one thing though. I don't miss radio."

"Why doesn't that surprise me?" says Johannes.

"I didn't realize until I was away from it what a deadly boring thing it was. Sitting in a room by yourself playing CDs. Ugh. At least this way I'm out among people."

"And only the best kind, too. By the by, I did a little etymological research on your behalf. You may be interested to know something I discovered about the word *paparazzi*. It comes from Fellini. Signor Paparazzo *in La Dolce Vita*. It's masculine in Italian. *Paparazzo*. I presume that makes you a *paparazza*."

"God I hope not."

"And you of all people of course know the translation. Don't you?"

"I guess I should. But no."

"You'll like this, hon. A *paparazzo* is a buzzing insect."

A woman with large breasts passes by on the sidewalk. "Why do they bounce like that?" says Johannes. "Is it the kind of support they wear? She was flopping."

Debra noticed too. She decides she'll play along with him. "It's the way she's walking probably more than anything."

"And she was giving me the eye, too."

"Have you ever slept with a woman?" asks Debra.

"With a breast? God no. Except my mother."

Debra says nothing.

"Now that I think of it," says Johannes, "I did sleep with a breast in college. We were both drunk and I guess she figured I was harmless, so she fell asleep on the bed next to me. Mother of Christ, when she woke up and realized — she went running for the bathroom. But I sure gave her a whuppin'."

Debra turns her head and looks up the sidewalk.

Johannes, suddenly bored with the conversation, drapes his arm over the back of the chair and does a pointed survey of the other customers, then turns back to Debra with a look of disgust and commiseration. "I see the *City Paper* crowd is out in force today. Poseurs, every one of them."

Debra recognizes this as the start of a long-standing diatribe that she and Johannes have shared, dating back to Johannes' bitter falling out with a former lover, a movie reviewer for the alternative newspaper.

"Here they are," Johannes continues, "striving desperately to be the very model of stylish eccentricity in dress, language, the foods they eat, in all they say and do, including naturally the manner in which they make love, etcetera, etcetera."

Debra empathizes, "And the movies they see."

"Yes, especially. They wind up forming one huge club of uniformity. How I do hate black clothing. Oh, and speaking of poseurs, did I mention who I saw here the other day? When was it? Tuesday."

Judging from the sudden vim in his voice Debra assumes Johannes has now arrived at the reason he extended this luncheon date in the first place.

"Your favorite arts administrator. She was bemoaning Be-More City's lack of outdoor cafes, even while sitting in one."

"I don't think I want to hear this," says Debra.

"Oh, you do, you do. There's no therapy quite like listening to a friend dis your enemy. It seems our darling Max – a name, I am told, that stems from a certain excess at an appointed time each month – "

"You're a dear, but you're trying too hard."

"Perhaps so. But isn't it pretty to think so. Anyway, anything for a friend. So, our darling Max has recently returned from gay Pair-ee where she discovered the mystical properties of outdoor cafes. I hear she had already name-dropped Deux-Magots before she got out of BWI. A Hemingway haunt, she says, as if I couldn't possibly have heard of it. She called it the nerve center for intellectuals, she of course being an intellectual's intellectual. So now back in our humble burg the culturally enlightened child is uttering things such as the notion that the French proudly consider themselves the most wicked people in the world, and she's finding it essential for her sense of self to sit here on the sidewalk for hours nursing a *cafe-creme* and playing dominos, all the while moralizing on the unhip. Have you seen her in her beret? She looks so – what? – *faux* something."

"Did she go with Donald?" Debra asks dryly. She and Donald had planned to travel one day to Paris.

She gets her answer from Johannes' evasive shrug.

"You don't know?" Debra says incredulously. "You're the one had lunch with her."

And with that the conversation stalls. A few minutes later Johannes says he has an appointment and puts enough money for not quite half the bill on the table. He starts to get up. "So what's your next exciting *paparazzi* adventure, Deb sweetie?"

"I don't know," she murmurs, annoyed. "I'll come up with something."

Johannes is all crinkly eyes and sardonic laugh lines. He tuts his tongue and says, "Very well, champagne wishes and caviar dreams."

*

Her new career gains momentum a few weeks later with her second exclusive tip. It comes on the phone from an old St. John's pal, Sean. Two years ago, Sean came into possession of a cache of old letters by and to the once-celebrated, long-reclusive silent-film actress Miss Georgia (pronounced GEOR-gee-ah) Brookins. The cache was so rich Sean secured a book contract to write her biography, conditional only on his getting the closed-mouth former sex symbol to talk about her page-boy past, especially the many *scandals d'amour* she is rumored to have carried on with figures of history – movie moguls, leading men, politicians, gangsters, and so on. This is Sean's first big break after years of miserable work in the Style section of a newspaper. He hopes it will allow him to quit the newspaper biz. But for two years the sour Miss Brookins has turned a deaf ear to Sean's obsequious entreaties, once even having him escorted by the police off the porch of her suburban St. Louis home. With each passing month she has grown feebler and Sean's publisher has grown more impatient. Finally, now that she is too sick to recover, Sean has given up hope – and upon giving up hope he has turned on Miss Brookins bitterly.

"I know where you can get her," says Sean. "She's dying of throat cancer in a convalescent hospital in St. Louis."

"A convalescent hospital?" says Debra. "How do I get a camera in *there*?"

"Walk in. Those places are open as train stations. Let me get you her current room number."

Debra flies to St. Louis. With her camera hidden in a glossy black Saks bag, she walks into the convalescent hospital, down a shiny and medicinal hallway, past nurses in rubber shoes, and directly into the room that contains Miss Brookins and two other women. At least it looks like it might be her. Debra checks the clipboard at the foot of the bed to be sure. Miss Brookins is shriveled nearly beyond recognition. Colorless. The line of her hair is nearly invisible against the white of her scalp. There are tubes in her arms and nostrils. The bed covers have been partly kicked off. Her sixty-pound frame is fetally curled.

Debra is repulsed, but she reminds herself she is here to do a job. She wastes no time. The N2000 clicks and whirs. When the old actress becomes vaguely aware of what's happening she manages to raise her withered hand just enough to shield her eyes. Debra draws close enough to smell her terminal, fecal breath, and pushes her hand down. She thinks she hears the old woman whisper, "No *paparazzi*."

The other patients, sitting up in bed, are too astonished to cry out – or too scared, or too fascinated. Anyway, they do nothing.

Debra has herself a $14,000 spread in *Celeb Search*: FORMER FLAPPER PRINCESS DYING AND ALONE. The same day she sees a grisly photo in *the New York Times* of four women weeping inconsolably on the steps of the State Supreme Court in lower Manhattan. The caption says they are family members of Yusef Rulaam, who has been convicted in a rape and murder trial. The photo credit reads: Art Buist/Reuters.

"I want you here, Ms. Infante," says the *Celeb Search* editor on the phone.

"Move to New York?"

"It's where the pictures are."

"I can't leave Baltimore," she says. "Not yet. I have friends here. I have a house."

Not that all her friends delight at her good fortune. As it happens, Miss Georgia Brookins is one of Johannes' silent film heartthrobs, right up there with Constance Talmadge and Norma Shearer. The day after Debra's *Celeb Search* spread hits the stands Johannes invites two dozen friends to his apartment for a Miss Georgia Brookins jamboree, during which they play Johannes' video of what is perhaps her greatest performance, "Beggar Girl in Silk Stockings." The next day he calls to tell Debra all about the party. "It's a pity you couldn't be there," says Johannes.

"So why didn't you invite me?" says Debra.

"Deb sweetie, don't think you were forgotten."

"Meaning what?"

"By the by, did I mention? Donald came. Not alone. They seem happy."

Debra says nothing. It's no secret that Max recently moved into Donald's new townhouse.

"You really do know how to hate, don't you, hon?" adds Johannes.

Debra stews on this conversation a few hours, then calls *the Celeb Search* editor and they make a deal. Thereafter, three times a week she takes a mid-morning train to New York for fourteen hours of squeezing into *paparazzi* lines shooting stars as they make their fleeting and scheduled appearances outside clubs and restaurants and at fashion benefits and theatre openings and weddings. The stars are obliging; no face is shielded. Debra's baby toilet flash is a hit with other *paparazzi*. It sets her apart from the crowd. She often sees Art Buist, who never fails to give her his wet, fleshy smile and ask her out for a drink. Finally, she goes.

Art Buist gestures to the bartender with bordello pimp savoir-faire and is served without ordering – some kind of drink with whisky and a splash of milk. Debra has "whatever's on tap." At the far end of the bar the TV chatters its mindless hilarity. A sit-com. Debra knows the names of all the actors, even the child bit-player.

After chatting up the bartender a few minutes, Art Buist turns to Debra and grows pensive over his drink. "I've been doing this twelve years." He sucks his teeth. "Never been a day when there wasn't work to be had if I wanted it. You don't shoot, you don't get paid."

"I'm shooting," says Debra, but then feels too confrontive and changes her tone. "Has it changed you after all these years?"

"I like that about you," says Art Buist, spreading his fingers on the bar like a fan. Sweaty hair clings to his forearm. "No question is too naive."

"Has it?"

"Changed me? As in, has it turned me into a gossip-rag whore?"

"Something like that."

"If that's what you're worried about, don't. You'll be who you are. But let me tell you. The number one rule out here is this. You're on the street. What you have here are situational ethics. When you go home, that's the time to be a caring individual. Out here, your job is to document your time. No picture, no document."

"Hmm," she says, looking down into her glass. She remembers that Art Buist's previous number one rule was don't touch someone else's camera. Two number one rules.

"I'm right you know. That's how I got to be who I am and where I am."

"As good as they get out here?"

"You can choose not to believe it, my little abandoned child. That doesn't make it less true." His pinkish eyelids flutter at her. "So are you coming home with me or what?"

Debra sips her beer thoughtfully. "My situational ethics tell me to string you along a while longer."

"Next time then."

Her pictures are published in nearly every issue of *Celeb Search*, usually without a credit, though she often lands the two-page clothes and cleavage spread WHAT PEOPLE ARE WEARING. Photos and Text by Debra Infante. *Boy oh boy! Supermodel Naomi Campbell must have used a shoehorn to get into this get-up!* With every click and whir of her N2000 she hears the sound of money.

She begins to subscribe to things in Donald's name, using Donald's credit card numbers, directing them to Donald's new address. Magazines by the dozen, book clubs, video clubs, CD clubs, scores of subscription forms. She pledges money to telethons for incurable diseases and public television fund drives, she takes out subscriptions of gourmet candies, beef, lingerie subscriptions – she doesn't care what those two do with it, so long as Donald understands that he is hated.

Then comes a day when Debra herself receives something interesting in the mail. An envelope marked PERSONAL AND CONFIDENTIAL is forwarded from *Celeb Search*. It is an unsigned letter saying that if Debra is willing to take a risk there is a way she can get pictures at the top celebrity wedding of the season, between the hysterically famous, misanthropic singer/performance artist Cassandra and her lover, the acerbic novelist Mr. Q. As all the world has been told, the ultra-private wedding is to take place in less than a week on Kiawah Island. A phone number is included.

The area code is somewhere in Iowa. Debra reaches a nervous young woman who won't give her name. "Don't bother trying to trace this call. I'm on a Firenze," she tells Debra.

"Trace it?"

"And if you reveal that I was the one who helped you they'll come after me. Swear on your mother's grave."

Debra's mother is alive and living a widow's life in Albany. Debra hasn't spoken with her since the day after Donald got off his semi-sick bed and left for good. Even that wasn't much of a conversation, just long enough to inform her of her daughter's new state of unmarriedness. "I swear on my mother's grave," says Debra. "Why are you doing this?"

"What's it to you?" says the young woman.

"I might need to know. You never know."

"Because I hate her to hell."

"Why?"

"It's true about you tabloid people, isn't it?"

"What?"

"You all stink to the core."

And thus is Debra reminded that the only real question, ever, is *How do I get in?*

"I have an invitation," says the young woman.

Next morning Debra receives, hand-delivered by messenger, a hand-engraved, gold leaf invitation to "The Wedding of the 90s."

CASSANDRA & MR. Q ARE GETTING MARRIED. THEY WANT YOU TO COME.

She buys a white linen Moschino suit and makes the drive to South Carolina, figuring that if there's to be some sort of *escape* she'd best not have to go through an airport. Wouldn't that be something, she thinks, a car chase off Kiawah Island.

Encamped outside the gate of the resort is a tabloid army. Boldly displayed on the sides of trucks are many of the biggest names in gossip: Hard Copy, A Current Affair, National Enquirer. There are satellite up-link trucks from ABC and Fox. Hot air balloons hang overhead. As she drives through the sprawling assemblage cameras are trained on her car.

She is stopped at the sentry post, but the invitation works like a magic key, opening the way to the opulent hideaway. The grounds are richly shaded by banyan, coconut palms and pine trees. Her tires crunch on the dried banyan leaves that carpet the narrow road. Signs warn STAY WELL CLEAR OF ALLIGATORS. THEY MOVE SWIFTLY AND ARE EXTREMELY DANGEROUS. She parks in a lot crowded with three dozen cars.

The wedding is to take place in a wood-frame villa nestled among the pines and oleander at the dunes' edge. At the entrance are two tuxedoed goons wearing shades and clear plastic ear pieces out of the back of their collars. They both give her a long look. Debra is carrying a large leather Fendi bucket bag. She's afraid they'll check it, but they don't.

A picture window the size of a drive-in movie screen looks out at the Atlantic at low tide. Debra is ushered to an aisle seat near the back where she can see everything. The whole affair is proper and sedate, with a conspicuous lack of celebs. Of the one-hundred or so guests, many, particularly on the bride's side, show an absence of hip.

Cassandra, whose performances are always fashioned around the day's hippest social holocaust and highlight her sexual parts, appears looking like the virgin bride in lace passementerie and a sheer, white La Sposa veil. Mr. Q, with too much gel in his almond brown hair, has zero presence next to her. It won't last, thinks Debra. A priest says Mass.

Debra watches for the right moment. She knows she'll get only a few shots before she has to bolt. The right moment comes once the happy couple have spoken their vows, kissed with showy passion, and are headed up the aisle. Cassandra's face is covered by the veil, but in the picture, there'll be no mistaking it's her. Debra steps into the aisle, the hard fist of her heart beating fast. She crouches low. The N2000 clicks and whirs furiously at the newlyweds. Mr. Q stops dead in his tracks and stiffens to rigid attention, but Cassandra takes to the attack, throwing back her veil and gesturing obscenely at the camera. She is cursing loudly – expletives strange and startling to Debra's not so tender ears. There is the most awful look in her eyes: rage, yes, but a rage that is other-worldly, and oddly projected several feet past where Debra is crouched. Stage rage. Her lipstick is black.

Debra shutters as she senses the tuxedoed goons fast approaching from either side. She leaps up to run but has mis-timed it. A goon grabs her arm and jerks it back, nearly unhinging her shoulder. With her free hand she holds the camera high and snaps him twice in the instant before the second goon seizes the camera and pulls her arm up behind, twisting in the socket. Cassandra approaches. Staring pointblank with that look of unreal rage, the superstar slaps her hard on the upper cheek, a fingernail flicking the corner of her eye. She calls Debra something so vulgar, so heart-piercing and sickening, it must surely be thrillingly new in the lexicon of hip obscenity.

Debra is led roughly away. Stiff with fear, she is certain the goons are going to hurt her badly. They take her directly to her car. One goon takes painful liberties with her breasts, then suddenly the leather strap of her satchel is around her throat and the goon chokes her with a hard yank. He shoves her face down on the hood. He has a fistful of her hair. He pounds her face once, twice. She glimpses her own blood smeared on the hood. She is jerked up by the hair and hurtled onto the grass in front of the car. Her eyes clouded, she is faintly aware of the other goon. He has her camera and is taking her picture. She looks up at him as he deftly unscrews the lens and smashes it beneath his heel. The first goon now grabs her under the arms and shoves her into the car. The other goon tosses her camera onto the passenger seat, and they walk away with a casual air.

Debra can hardly raise her arms to grip the steering wheel. She drives slowly off the resort, through the tabloid army outside the gate. Her vision is curdled by tears and a tremendous pain in the center of her face. She nearly hits a man with three cameras around his neck who has stepped in front of the car trying to take her picture; slamming the brakes. When she finally gets off the island and reaches the turn-off to Hwy 17 she stops and breaks down in a terrible cry. In the rearview mirror she sees her nose is swelling right before her eyes. Her white linen suit is scuffed with grass stains and spotted with specks of blood. She checks her camera and finds the film still inside.

Back in her basement darkroom, watching the pictures develop, she squeals with delight and it hurts her impacted nose.

"Congratulations, chosen one," says the *Celeb Search* editor, who is paying beaucoup for all twenty-one shots, including the two slightly unfocused, over-the-shoulder shots of the goon. Even the one of her sprawled on the grass. "Cassandra's provided you a seat at the table. Get an agent."

"Why'd she pick me?" says Debra.

"I prefer to think she picked the magazine, pumpkin."

Debra is too pleased with herself to let her broken nose get her down. Besides, she's got plenty from the Cassandra shoot to find the best surgeon in Manhattan, when she wants. For now, she's staying home to heal, and decides that if she's going to do this *paparazzi* gig on a long-term basis she'd better get even better acquainted with her subjects. She becomes a couch potato. The TV is on all day. She reads magazines and tabloids, sharpening her (blackened) eye for who's hot and who's not, memorizing names and faces. All her life she selected from popular culture with a connoisseur's eye. Now she wallows in it. A student of her own culture. *Woman Loses 150 lbs. by Eating Candy.* She puts her hair in the new "updo." *Feel Better by Complaining. Stories about Jacko. Runway Report: Belgian Blonde Bombshell Supermodel. What Hollywood Stars Will Not Eat!* She takes the TV Fun Quiz and nails all twenty Qs. *Hubby Kept Wife Like a Prisoner in the*

Basement. She whips up some of Erik Estrada's "Instant Flan." Everyone is cheating on the spouse, or not cheating and declaring monogamy. "Get used to it: From Courtney to couture, lingerie is here to stay. The trick to boudoir dressing now? Make it your own." *Startling Secrets Revealed!* (in every issue).

"It's so yucky," Debra says to herself. She spots photos by Art Buist in five different mags. She regains all her weight with pounds to spare. After three weeks her head is crammed full of junk culture and she is ready to give it a rest.

She returns to Taube's to buy another camera and winds up buying three. She can certainly afford it. Taube admits he has not been following her *paparazzi* career. He seems a little surprised she is still at it. She tells him about Kiawah Island. "I have the pictures and the nose to prove it."

"I'm teaching a class at Towson State," says Taube. "Maybe you could stop in one week and talk with the students."

"What kind of class is it?"

"An introduction."

"I don't know. I'd feel self-conscious talking about photography in front of you," she says. "Especially technical things. What could I say?"

Taube has the mischievous look she saw before in him. She can't tell if he's making fun of her. "Some of these kids think they want to be photographers – for a living," he says. You can tell them about a side of the business that I can't. I won't ask you to talk about reciprocity failure. Nor will they."

She tells him she'll think about it, but leaves the store feeling vaguely embarrassed and wondering if she will be back. She has everything she needs from Taube. She can buy paper and chemicals at another store. She has promised to send him her Cassandra pictures, but by the time she gets in her car she knows she won't.

At home she suddenly has a strong desire to read something that is utterly without practical application. She picks from the shelves an oversized photo book called *Monuments of Civilization: EGYPT*. Donald must have left it behind. She opens it at random and reads this: "Much has been written about the relations between Queen Hatshepsut and Senmut, her chief and most trusted minister, and even today there are some who search for spicy details, as if it were a case for sensational journalism. In fact, all the extant documentation on these two illustrious personages is strictly official; no ancient Egyptian would dream of recording his private affairs in an official document, least of all a queen. In any case, none of this gossip matters from a historical point of view."

Next day, she's about to leave the house to indulge herself in a CD buying spree (lately she's had a craving for Chopin and Ravel), when the *Celeb Search* editor calls with a tip she's received about Tom Gunner, TV's first heavy metal detective, star of the top-rated ABC adventure-romance series

Hardass. Or former star. Several weeks ago, after shooting the final episode of his third season, Gunner shocked his fans and the industry alike by quitting. "Tom Gunner wants to pursue other avenues in his career," he announced at a press conference. He disappeared for an extended vacation and has not been spotted since. Rumors have been flying.

"I got a joker in D.C.'s trying to sell me a stack of Polaroids of someone he claims is Gunner," says the *Celeb Search* editor. "Says Gunner's living up the street in some tumbledown, pissed to the bushy eyebrows. Normally I'd tell him to bite it, but these... I would say it looks like our swarthy Sgt. Hardass all right, less the hair."

"Yeah?" says Debra.

"So you're going down there in the morning to do a professional job of it."

Next morning, Debra stakes out in her car on an unshaded street which has been touched many times by vandals, across from a house with a rotten porch and stains on the walls, and windows covered with black painted cardboard. She keeps the car locked. She slouches low against the passenger door, wrapped in a blanket. In the tedium she eats her entire bag of food in the first five hours. She dozes and wakes with a start when the car rattles from a train passing a block away. Her lower back aches. She keeps slugging down Tylenol for the pain in her nose and forehead. Questions of amazement slowly form in the cold air inside the car. Why would a man do this? What terrible thing could have happened to him? Why did he come *here*?

And these questions are soon followed by others familiar to Debra, gelatinous questions that for months she has persistently choked back. Why is *she* here? For too long she has felt an odd blank feeling. She's been aware of just going through the motions, albeit skillfully. She seeks out her subject, gets her picture, is professional about it, makes few mistakes. The last months, she's watched with only small curiosity as she's made her way by taking pictures – no, taking *these* pictures. She usually is faintly startled upon feeling a perverse mixture of revulsion and helpless attraction. This is strongest when her subjects object to having their picture taken. But it is her job. She does not allow herself an upwelling of sympathy or arguments of ethics. At times like these, of reflection, she tells herself to wake up and see things straight. She remembers Art Buist.

As the moon's frail light falls upon the street, Debra is thinking that maybe Tom Gunner isn't in the house after all. There's been no lights, no movement. She calls it a day.

Next morning, she arrives at 7:15 and before she can even get the top off her thermos, here comes her man walking up the sidewalk, a paper sack tucked in close at the elbow. He is waxen and stooped, but it is him: Tom Gunner, heavy metal detective. What a sight! His hair – once the sexiest Aerosmith do on the tube – is short and dirt brown.

What a deliciously pitiful sight! She rolls down the window and nails Tom Gunner several times before he lifts his uncomprehending eyes. She turns on the ignition and is prepared for a screeching getaway, but Tom Gunner raises his hand and makes a negligible gesture her way and turns his back and walks toward the house. She nails him twice more from the side.

GUNNER DESTITUTE IN D.C.!

Then, incredibly, Debra's fortunes multiply two days after *Celeb Search* scores its fabulous exclusive coup. TV star Tom Gunner is busted for buying crack from an undercover cop. "Nothing like credibility," says the *Celeb Search* editor. In the next issue *Celeb Search* is running two more from her D.C. shoot, and three others have been selling fast to wire services and syndicates throughout the world. "*Pravda* wants in," exclaims the editor. "It's payday."

"Wow," says Debra.

Three weeks later, she goes back out on the *paparazzi* lines and is aware that she has risen in the estimation of her colleagues. She can feel it in the way others follow her movements. She sees it in their grudging smiles. Art Buist puts his arm around her shoulder and gives her a sweaty hug. He introduces her around as the girl who landed Cassandra and Gunner. These are big game they have only dreamed of. She looks into the faces of the most veteran *paparazzi*, looking for signs of her future. But she cannot decide what she sees. They show a certain nervous aggression, true, but not so much like buzzing insects as like associate professors back at St. John's hustling in the hallways for tenure votes. They look no more heartless or unhappy than anyone else.

Then comes *l'ultima foto*. One night she is lying across her bed tweezing her eyebrows, when she gets a phone call from the Baltimore Police. There's been a fatal car accident. The car was in flames. The body has been badly disfigured, but the police have good reason to think it is her soon-to-be-legally-ex-husband. They need a positive identification.

"Huh?" says Debra. She thinks this is something for Max to see. She's about to give the cop Max's name but thinks otherwise.

"We can have a car there to escort you to the hospital, Miss, if you'd prefer," says the cop.

"Uh...no. Where is it?"

So, on the drive to the hospital morgue, with her Fendi bucket bag on the seat beside her, does Debra wrestle with her intentions? Does she swallow the vengeful glob in her throat? Does she recall with sad fondness her years of marital harmony and wholeness, like flowers pressed in a book? Does she think: "The man is dead, let it rest?"

The morgue attendant peels back the thick plastic cover, and it *is* Donald, lying in a metal drawer, his face incinerated, his great orange mane singed to ringlets no bigger than pencil shavings. It is recognizably and undeniably Donald Woodwell.

"Could I have a moment alone with him?" asks Debra. "I was his wife."

"Certainly." He steps back.

No, on the drive to the morgue Debra does none of that. On principle. Hers is unceasing forward momentum. *Vendetta*, she tells herself, is a feminine noun.

The camera clicks and whirs. This time it is not the sound of money she hears. She's thinking of something else. She's thinking she knows the perfect place to hang these new B & Ws of Donald.

Made in the USA
Coppell, TX
19 September 2020